The Women on the Bridge

The Women on the Bridge

Mel Dagg

Thistledown Press Ltd.

Dagg, Mel, 1941-

The women on the bridge

ISBN 0-920633-99-4

I. Frog Lake (Alta.) - History - Massacre, 1885 -
Fiction.* I. Title

PS8557.A26W44 1992   C813'.54   C92-098114-3
PR9199.3.D25W44   1992

Book design by A.M. Forrie
Cover art by David Alexander - Acrylic on canvas - 60 x 68 cm - 1989
Map by Scott Cumberland
Typeset by Thistledown Press Ltd.

Printed and bound in Canada by
Kromar Printing Ltd.
725 Portage Ave.
Winnipeg, Manitoba R3G 0M8

Thistledown Press Ltd.
668 East Place
Saskatoon, Saskatchewan S7J 2Z5

Acknowledgements

This book has been published with the assistance of The Canada Council and
the Saskatchewan Arts Board.

I am grateful to The Canada Council and the Alberta Foundation for the Literary Arts for grants received during the researching and writing of this work.

The title story, "The Women on the Bridge", was broadcast on CBC's "Alberta Anthology".

I would like to thank Glen Sorestad for his encouragement and patience as an editor. I also wish to thank Jennifer Bobrovitz, Local History Librarian, Calgary Public Library, for her invaluable research assistance and advice.

The stories in this collection are a work of fiction, though the events and most of the characters are historical.

Mel Dagg
June 1992

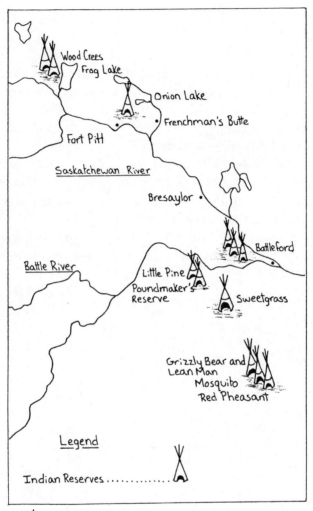

Wood Crees
Frog Lake
Onion Lake
Frenchman's Butte
Fort Pitt
Saskatchewan River
Bresaylor
Battleford
Battle River
Little Pine
Poundmaker's Reserve
Sweetgrass
Grizzly Bear and Lean Man
Mosquito
Red Pheasant

Legend

Indian Reserves . . . .

Saskatchewan Territories

CONTENTS

THE SOUND AT THE END OF THE STREET

Fort Macleod, Summer 1884

Harry Kamouse Taylor took out his bible and had his first drink of the day. The country was "dry," so Taylor drank from a tin flask inscribed HOLY BIBLE and filled with special stock smuggled up from Fort Benton. Kamouse was a nickname given Taylor in the old days by the Blackfoot, an acknowledgement of the past they shared before Taylor became the respectable owner of the only hotel in Fort Macleod. It meant *thief* in Blackfoot.

Taylor pressed the flask to his lips, tilted his head to take a drink, and the prairie sun caught the shock of white eyebrows arching over hard steel-blue bloodshot eyes set in the face of a man living in the hell he and his whiskey-trading partner, Al B. Hamilton, spread among the Blackfoot. Taylor lowered his head, corked the flask, and waited for the first merciful wave of whiskey to hit him.

Lately he had been hearing a strange sound he could never track down. Some days it was like musical notes tumbling at random; other times it was the clatter of dice in a tumbler, the chink of a spoon against a cup, or the rattle of his own death. Taylor took another nip to smooth the edges and muffle the noise that wouldn't go away.

Odd, life's little turns. Before the business of swindling Indians out of buffalo robes for bad whiskey he tried preaching. But it wasn't nearly so profitable. Preaching and whiskey: seemed somewhat fitting to drink from a tin bible, so he had another and then eased comfortably back in his chair. Dissolving in whiskey and the warmth of the sun, Harry Kamouse Taylor waited for the stage to arrive.

Right on time too, he thought, listening with his eyes half-closed to the trundling rattle of its approach. He opened his eyes and saw spoked wooden wheels stilled, horses idle and shuddering in the heat. A voice called down to him from the driver's seat, "Here's yer mail, Harry!"

A small bundle of papers tumbled to the boardwalk at Taylor's feet as the driver stirred his team and the creak of harness and clop of horses faded down the street to the stables at the far end of town.

Now that the whiskey was working Taylor considered the arrival of the stage a sign that the day was unfolding as it should. He was just bending to pick up his papers when the noise resumed with maddening clarity. Clutching the papers to his chest Taylor staggered into the street; he had to find the source of that sound.

It was coming from the stables, or the blacksmith shop adjoining the stables. Yet it wasn't the clang of hot red steel ringing on an anvil, but more muffled, hollow, empty, the chink of tile or clatter of bones, someone piling dry kindling, louder behind the stables. His free hand holding the rough timber of the building for support, cautiously, inch by inch he moved along the wall that ended at the rear corner of the building where he turned into the blinding glare of three mountains of bleached white buffalo bones. There was no escape from the brightness of the noon-day sun on the bones as Taylor clung to the back wall of the stable and listened to the sound of them being dumped.

The horse had blinders on. An old man walked the single horse cart toward the middle pile of bones, leading the horse by the harness. He shuffled to the rear, tipped the cart, and an avalanche of skulls, backbones, and ribs tumbled out at Taylor's feet.

"Welcome to the boneyard, Harry!"

He turned to see the young man who kept the stables and dealt in horses. "Can't you do something about this noise?" he asked.

"Why Harry, them bones make the sweetest sound in the world, the sound of money being made."

"No," said Taylor. "You don't understand."

"Why, it's the comin' thing!" interrupted the young man. "Everyone's gettin' in on it. Farmers, kids, even Indians. Pickin' the plains clean. Use em' in fertilizer, glue, sugar refining. Make a fine button or comb. Every time I hear the clatter of that cart unloading's like countin' money in the bank. Nine dollars a ton I get and I got every reason to believe the price will double 'cause they use the potassium in the bones to make gun powder."

Taylor lurched against the side of the building, lifted the flask to his lips, and quickly drained it. "What you talkin' 'bout?"

"Ain't you heard? Everyone knows Crozier had to break in on a Sun Dance and arrest two Indians. Wouldn't give themselves up. Turned into a stand-off between the police and Big Bear'n Poundmaker's men. Why it's all over that newspaper you got in your hand. Battleford's preparing for the worst."

Taylor stared into the young man's lean face and saw himself years ago as a young whiskey trader. He'd tell him a thing or two, set him straight. He moved from the wall waving his newspaper in one hand, the empty flask in the other, when the whiskey, the heat, and the walk hit him hard.

Reeling in the heat, he staggered into the glare of noon-day sun and stumbled among the bleached buffalo bones. "Gone," he muttered. "All gone!"

He hurled the flask at the sightless black sockets of the skulls and the empty echo of tin bounced off the bones. His legs were giving out under him. The stablekeeper ran up the street for help, Taylor sank crashing into the bones.

Two men, one on either side, were pulling him by the arms, the heels of his boots dragging across the bones.

"Look," someone said, as the men dragged Taylor back to his hotel. "Ole man Taylor's got one leg in the bag this early in the day!"

But as Taylor jerked and danced a spastic shuffle between the two men, he heard nothing but the chink and clatter of buffalo bones calling him to his death.

He awoke in a sweat and slowly raised himself up in bed. It was very still in the room, as if time had stopped. An old Indian woman sat at the window, her back to him, a shawl covering her shoulders. Taylor recognized the shawl, once red but faded now to rust brown, and the woman wearing it. Then his head sank back onto the pillow and the room began to swirl.

Trapped in a room in his own hotel, Taylor floated through time in fevered hallucination, slipping in and out of a coma. Old friends came and went, their visits confused with the clarity with which his life passed before him in a series of intense tableaux. Clear and real as if he were right in the room with him Taylor heard the voice of his partner plot his scheme to sell liquor to the Indians.

"I got us a layout far superior to robbin' stages and not near so risky. I offer you the once-in-a-lifetime opportunity to join with me and my Fort Benton associate, Sheriff John Healy, to become pioneers of commerce and free enterprise on the Canadian frontier."

Hamilton lifted the lid off a black kettle under which a fire roared and sniffed the concoction within. "Needs a touch more body," he concluded, upending a crock of black-strap molasses into the kettle. "This here molasses'll make them Cree up north think they's drinkin' Hudson's Bay rum!"

He dumped a quart of whiskey, a pound of chewing tobacco, some hot red pepper, and a bottle of ginger into the kettle. Then Hamilton handed Taylor an empty bottle of Perry's Pain Killer, the principle ingredient of which was opium. "Never let it be said we dealt in shoddy goods or sold an inferior product!"

Hamilton's voice faded away and other sounds filled Taylor's room, some actual, some dreamt, all real: horses pawed along the narrow ledge of a mountain trail, their hesitant hooves dislodging small stones that tumbled noisily into the canyon below on the night Taylor and Hamilton first moved their whiskey across the border, fifteen years ago. Now those same loosened rocks tumbled through Taylor's dreams at night and in the morning he awoke to the sound outside his window of buffalo bones being stockpiled behind the stable.

He had tried to forget, to take the money made trading buffalo robes for whiskey and become a respectably eccentric innkeeper, but his past was alive in the bones. Unmistakable in its austere finality, the message in the dry bones tumbled out of the old man's cart: he, Taylor, was responsible for the mountains of bones rising behind the town.

The woman had been in Taylor's room for months now, ever since he had collapsed in the buffalo bones. She hated the town, the way they looked at her. "Taylor's squaw," they called her. She watched his frail head thrash from side to side on his sweaty pillow as he tried to pull himself out of wherever he was.

"Hush," she whispered, placing her hand on his hot forehead. "You must forget this thing that has taken hold of you. It does no good to remember."

Taylor watched her take a braided plait of sweet-grass from her bag, yellow as hay and streaked with green. The braid narrowed to a fine point at the end. She held it over the flame from the lamp.

"I will burn this sweet-grass to make you forget," she muttered, more to herself than to Taylor.

Smoke from the glowing tips of the braided sweet-grass filled the room. Taylor started to cough. *Why*, he thought, *she is trying to burn me out!*

But when his coughing subsided he realized the room was not on fire and squinting through the smoke he saw the woman walk across the room toward the door. He sat up in bed, watching her body move beneath the folds of her loose faded cotton dress as her moccasined feet padded across the wooden floor. Her brown hand closed around the white porcelain doorknob.

"Don't leave," he said. "Not now."

"I am not leaving," she said. "I am only opening the door, and when I do, the people you thought were here in your room talking with you, one by one, they will leave. There will be no one here but you and me."

She crossed the room and raised the window. A draft connecting with the open door was drawing the sweet-grass smoke from the room. Taylor watched the heavy incense of the sweet-grass drift out through the door. In the curling shape of the incense, palpable in the last shifting wisp of smoke, he watched the figure of Al B. Hamilton slip from the room.

"It's you, isn't it?"

"Yes," she said, sitting in the chair at his bedside. "It is me. It is only the years that have made me this way: years living without the buffalo, years on the reservation, begging the Farm Instructor for bad flour and bacon. Do you know I had to plead for written permission to leave the reservation just to come and visit you?"

"I'm sorry," said Taylor. "Truly sorry." It was all he could think of to say. "Do you hear that noise?" he asked.

"It is not the noise that bothers you but its meaning," she said. "And that cannot be as bad as the sound of those bones are to me. I cannot make the noise go away. Why don't you read your newspapers? Some children brought them to me after they carried you in here. You must have dropped them. It'll take your mind off the noise."

As she left the room Taylor reached for the newspaper and the headline caught and held him.

THE INDIAN TROUBLE

HEROIC CONDUCT OF POLICE

HARMONY AGAIN PREVAILS

"Harmony again prevails," Taylor read out loud, but from the far end of the street the cold chink of the accumulating buffalo bones made his hands shake so badly the small print of the *Saskatchewan Herald* was impossible to read.

He placed the paper on the bed and hunched over it so he could read without holding it in his trembling hands. He had to find out what was going on. The writing was so biased and inflammatory that no matter how many times Taylor read the account he still couldn't tell what had happened. Repeatedly the newspaper credited Crozier with avoiding armed conflict.

> The country owes a debt of gratitude to Major Crozier for his patience and the tact displayed, and to the men of the force for their coolness in the face of danger.

Taylor moved across the bed and parted the curtain to let in more light. He stared out the window across the flat alluvial plain at the garrisoned cluster of buildings on the delta-like island in the middle of Old Man River. Fort Macleod. There, in the first Mounted Police post built in the North-West, Crozier cut his teeth on the country, closing down whiskey traders like Taylor.

He turned back to his newspapers, sifting through the prose for a few facts. Two Cree, it seemed, got into an argument with a Farm Instructor named John Craig over a sack of flour and the incident escalated into a four-day face-off between the police and the combined bands of Big Bear and Poundmaker. The *Herald* article ended by calling for a militia, uniforms, and a rehearsal for war:

The government went to a great deal of trouble to send the offscourings of the plains over here, where they would be out of the way; they must now continue their efforts to prevent their continuing to be a nuisance. Recent events in this district ought to lead Sir John Macdonald to have effective volunteer companies organized in every settlement in the country.

He set the newspaper aside. The tone of the article reminded him of the young stablekeeper. Taylor was sober, sitting up in bed, and thinking how it was all wrong, terribly wrong, when the door opened and the Indian woman entered.

She looked nothing like the woman he once knew. Her aged wrinkled face peered into his.

"Do you remember?" he asked, for there was nothing left to lose now.

"Yes," she said. "I will always remember." She parted the coarse fabric of the curtain and stared into the dim haze of the distant mountains. "We were free and wild and so was the country."

She looked down on the littered street of the town below. "But now your numbers swell and you push us onto the reservation. My people are out there, beyond your town, and I must be with them, not here." She bent to lift the window. "Listen," she said. "Do you hear it? It will not go away. Face it as I have had to face it. It is what we have become."

Ten miles south of the buffalo jump where the herds stampeded to their deaths, the man and woman in the hotel room listened to the sound of bones being gathered at the far end of the town. Faintly musical, the sound floated up from the street and through the open window, filling the room, the chink and clatter of buffalo bones, part of the accumulating madness afflicting the country.

A SACK OF FLOUR

Near Poundmaker's Reserve
Summer, 1884

On horseback, wagon, and on foot, by mid-June sixteen hundred men, women, and children, moving into the valley of the Battle River. Big Bear, at Poundmaker's invitation, was sponsoring a Thirst Dance. There would be a Grand Council of Chiefs.

The Indian Department's policy of keeping the Cree on small, separate reserves, and of keeping Big Bear in the Frog Lake District, was falling apart. Rumours of an uprising began to circulate in Battleford, and Crozier ordered Corporal R.B. Sleigh and six men to observe the Thirst Dance camp closely.

Corporal Sleigh's telescope swept across the tipis and focused finally on the larger lodges in the centre: a man wearing the skinned head of a coyote riding a cream-coloured horse painted with symbols of some kind. Thirty, no, he counted forty men riding toward the trees bordering the river. Older men following on foot, chanting.

Paint-streaked men were gathering around the chosen tree, raising their guns to the sky. Rifle shots burst across the valley. A blue haze of powder smoke drifted up as the tree wavered, slanted out of the sky, and crashed to the earth.

Sleigh thought they must have been chopping just before the shots were fired. Now they were trimming the tree, limbing it, men with ropes tied to their saddles ready to drag it to camp.

Yes, Sleigh reflected, folding away his telescope. That's how it was done. They began chopping *before* the shots were fired. Yet he hadn't heard the axes. Next time he would notice. And even as he thought this, suddenly thankful for Crozier's assignment, he realized he would never again get a chance to observe a Thirst Dance so closely. He must catch each detail of the ritual unfolding below him.

Seated on the hilltop with Robert Jefferson, the Farm Instructor on Poundmaker's Reserve, Sleigh caught only a glimpse of the energies that were sweeping through the societies, the councils, the camp: Lone Man, in from the south with a herd of captured horses, started the storytellers; Fine Day told of a raid on the Sioux when he was sixteen. In the telling they forgot the poverty and hunger that gripped the camp. The young men listened, grasping at the glory their elders had known, the pride denied them in the present.

While Big Bear withdrew to pray and prepare for the Thirst Dance, two young men — The Clothes, and Man Who Speaks Our Language — rode out from the camp to scour the countryside for food. After riding for several hours they found themselves on Little Pine's reserve.

The place was deserted, with everyone gone to the Thirst Dance, quiet and still, except for the sounds of something dragging across the floor of the white man's storeroom. Man Who Speaks Our Language and The Clothes rode quietly toward the sounds coming from the storeroom, dismounted, and slipped inside.

The Farm Instructor, an American named John Craig, wheeled to face two young Cree demanding food in a language he neither understood nor spoke. Still, he had his orders from Agent Rae: no rations for Indians taking part in the Thirst Dance. The two Cree wanted a sack of flour for their families. Craig stood his ground. "Get out!" he shouted.

Man Who Speaks Our Language and The Clothes studied Craig's angry gestures, listened to him shout in his strange language, but decided not to leave. History comes down to this: within the walls of a small shed, two Plains Cree and a white government official squabble over a sack of flour.

Craig shoved Man Who Speaks Our Language hard on the chest, pushing the surprised Cree to the door when the warrior's hands, which so far he had restrained from placing on Craig, his right hand reaching behind him into a barrel by the door, closed on the familiar feel of an axe handle. He arced the axe handle over his shoulder, and slicing the moving edge of the lethal weapon through the sudden silence, brought the handle down on Craig, but at the last moment, held back, tapping him lightly on the arm.

A *coup*, nothing more. Craig had shoved him, so he would touch the white man with a *coup* stick, let him know his limits, the possibilities. The axe handle clattered to the floor at Craig's feet; the two Cree backed out of the storeroom.

The Farm Instructor stood in the open doorway, checked, humiliated, seething with rage. His arm stung, not so much from physical pain but from the knowledge of what had happened. They'd be taught a lesson or he was finished on this reserve. "You'll pay for this!" he shouted. "You'll both be in irons before the day ends!"

But Man Who Speaks Our Language and The Clothes did not understand Craig. They rode back to the Thirst Dance talking of how they would tell of the *coup* taken from the Farm Instructor.

From the hill Sleigh and Jefferson watched the Thirst Dance lodge rise below them. The horsemen who brought in the pole ate berries while two elders led each rider to a young woman. The women rode double with the men through the camp, singing, then rode off to bring back the rafters and timbers for the Thirst Dance lodge.

Men came forward and hung offerings from the centre-pole: guns, clothing, spirit powers. They dropped cloth and burning sweetgrass into the hole until it was ready at last to receive the pole, the men pulling on ropes, the pole rising into the air, the men steadying it.

"They've got it up," Sleigh observed. "I say, Jefferson, they've got it up!"

"Look," said Jefferson, pointing.

Across the valley trails of dust billowed behind riders dragging downed trees toward the Thirst Dance camp from all directions. Sleigh and Jefferson watched young men and girls bring in the rafters and place them out from the boughs of the Thunderbird nest in four directions.

Jefferson and Sleigh were settling into a summer afternoon watching the Thirst Dance preparations below them when they were startled by someone riding in on them hard. John Craig jumped from his horse and strode toward them, yelling, gesturing, seeming to come quite undone. He opened his mouth to speak and instead gasped in air.

"For God's sake, what is it?" asked Sleigh.

Craig staggered to the crest of the hill and pointed down at the Thirst Dance camp. "Attack!" he gasped. "Attacked by two bloody Indians down there! Came at me with an axe handle. Arrest them!"

"Sit down, man," urged Sleigh. "Tell us what happened."

Craig crumpled to the ground and blurted his story. "Come upon me while I was taking inventory in the storehouse. Two of them, demanding food. I don't speak Cree and I'm damn sure they don't speak English. Well, they wouldn't go. Just stood there, the two of them, defying me. So I shoved them. Had to get rid of them, didn't I? Well, that's when one of them whacked me on the arm with an axe handle."

"Let's see your arm, then," said Sleigh.

Craig rolled his shirt sleeve up to his elbow and thrust his arm out at Sleigh. Halfway between his wrist and elbow a reddening welt was forming on the surface of his skin that, it occurred to Sleigh, could have been caused by almost anything. "Are you hurt?" he asked.

"That's not the point, Corporal. I'm filing charges of assault and it's the duty of the police to arrest them two."

"Are you sure this is all really necessary?" asked Sleigh. "After all, you don't seem injured in any way."

"Injured? Dammit man! Word gets out them two bucks bested me in my own storehouse my position as Instructor on Little Pine will be worthless."

"It is anyway," muttered Jefferson.

"You stay out of this, Jefferson!" Craig shouted. "This is a matter for the police."

"Surely you don't expect me to go down there with six men and make the arrest, Craig? My orders are to observe the Thirst Dance encampment."

"I want those men arrested!" insisted Craig. "They've got to be taught a lesson."

"Very well," snapped Sleigh. "I'll send a man to Battleford with a message for Superintendent Crozier."

Craig paced, unsatisfied, anxious for vindication. Sleigh had half a mind to send him to Battleford with his own complaint, just to work it off, but then thought better of it and decided to send one of his own men.

"Sanders," he said. "Ride to Battleford and inform Superintendent Crozier that Farm Instructor Craig claims he was assaulted by two Indians and demands their arrest. That is all, Sanders. Better get going. It's almost nightfall and it's a long ride to Battleford."

And for a few moments, walking through the slow-turning dusk toward the small figure of Jefferson silhouetted on the crest of the hill – Jefferson, who worked so hard and so well with Poundmaker and his people – Sleigh allowed himself to believe they had heard the last of Craig.

"Too bad about this Craig business," he said as he rejoined Jefferson. "Still, I expect it'll blow over."

But when he stared into the valley of small fires and moving shadows he wasn't so sure. Drums throbbed in the gathering darkness, joined by the long undulating chant of singers that rose and fell on the insistent beat, and over this, a third layer of sound, shrill, like a chorus of piping birds, the hollowed-out leg bone of a goose pressed to the lips of each dancer, blown to the beat of the drum. The dancing had begun. They would dance all night. It would not stop until the camp disbanded days from now. This Craig thing could turn like that. Now that it had started it might not stop until it had run its course.

Sometime before noon a single column of red moved out of the distant heat haze of the hills and separated as it neared into individual riders, Inspector Antrobus and Superintendent Crozier at the head of thirty police.

Craig repeated his story for Crozier. During the night Craig had been busy distributing favours for information and had it on good authority his two assailants were among the dancers in the Thirst Dance lodge directly below the hill. They had let it be known they would not be taken prisoner.

Crozier listened until Craig got to the part about his two assailants being among the dancers in the Thirst Dance lodge. He looked down the hill at the men that bobbed and circled to the beat of the drum and said, "If they're among the dancers, that's right where we want them. Effect an arrest quickly. Take them by surprise. We'll ride right in and while my men remain mounted as back-up, Craig, myself and Sleigh will dismount, walk quickly into the Thirst Dance lodge where Craig can identify his men and we make the arrest. I want a quick solution to this matter before it gets out of hand. *Remember, timing is everything.* Move in quickly, don't falter, and we'll have them.

"Jefferson, you come along as interpreter. It should come off smoothly, but I want someone there who speaks the language."

Jefferson joined Crozier, Craig, and Sleigh in the front of the column. Counting Sleigh's original six, thirty-six police moving, awkward and slow down the hillside into the Indian encampment. The drums and the chant and cries of the camp grew louder.

"Looks like you'll get to see your Thirst Dance after all!" Jefferson called to Sleigh.

Suddenly Crozier raised his hand and the entire column came to a halt.

"Excuse me, gentlemen," said Crozier. "This will only take a minute." He undid his tunic, took it off, and folded it neatly over his saddle. "Wouldn't do to wear one of these all the way up from Battleford in this heat," said Crozier, slipping his arms through a heavy black cloth vest into which were sewn thin plates of spring steel, one on either side of his chest.

"Repeatedly and thoroughly tested with rifle bullets at forty yards," Crozier tapped the steel with his knuckle and began buttoning the vest, the steel plates overlapping in the centre. "This is the officer's model."

Crozier walked stiffly to his horse, took his tunic from his saddle, put it on, and buttoned it up over the bullet-proof vest. Then he hefted himself up into the saddle.

At the bottom of the hill Crozier's men broke formation, their mounts weaving between the tipis toward the roar that throbbed in the beating centre of the camp. The chiefs did not come out to meet them; not a man nor woman approached them.

A six-foot hide wall shielded the Thirst Dance participants from the view of the camp. The wall shook to the drumming and chanting of the dance within, as if the stretched skin of the shield wall enclosure was itself a drum. Sleigh glanced up at the Thunderbird nest in the open-to-the-sky roof.

The mounted company of police waited while Sleigh, Crozier, Jefferson and Craig stood together for a moment. "Come along, Craig," Crozier snapped. "Let's see if we can find your men." Crozier and Sleigh pushed through the armed Indians and the four men thrust themselves into the Thirst Dance lodge.

Their faces and bodies smeared with paint and clay, the Cree men moved to the beat of the drum, blew goose bone whistles to the rhythm of their steps, and completely ignored the four white men staring at them.

"Well?" shouted Crozier, the noon summer sun on the steel breast-plate under his wool tunic working him into a sweat.

Craig was silent.

Transfixed, Sleigh stared up into the great ball of noon sun burning through the Thunderbird's hoary nest of cloth, blankets, rifles and hanging leather bags. Under the very centre-pole he had watched being raised yesterday, Sleigh now stood at the heart of an incredible throbbing energy.

His eyes dropped from the sun to the circle of moving dancers. A human mandala of arched moccasined feet touched the earth to the beat of the drum; separate, the women danced on the other side of a barrier of boughs. This was the inner circle in which neither he nor any white man could step.

"Dammit man!" shouted Crozier. "Can you make your identification or not?"

"I can't be sure," said Craig. "I just can't be sure. With paint streaked on their faces they all look the same."

Crozier's face fell. Craig couldn't make the identification. He had drawn Crozier into a deadly game, into the very centre of the Indian camp, where the police superintendent was watching his plan for a quick arrest fall apart. Sweat streamed down Crozier's armoured chest and soaked through his tunic.

Drums pounded in his head as the dancers circled, mocking him, it seemed.

"If you can't identify them, Mr. Craig, I suggest we get out of this insanity!" shouted Crozier.

Caught up in the ritual, watching the dancers, Sleigh felt someone tugging at his sleeve. "We're leaving," Jefferson told him.

Sleigh stood still, staring into the circle of dancers. "C'mon man!" shouted Jefferson. "We're leaving. I suggest we do it as a group."

The four men forced their way past the ring of observers, out of the Thirst Dance lodge, and into an angry taunting mob. "They're in there," insisted Craig. "I know they are."

"Lot of good that does us, if you don't recognize them," Crozier shouted. "I suggest you forget for a moment where your two precious Indians are, Mr. Craig, and instead, be mindful of where *we* are!"

"What do we do now?" asked Craig.

"Keep moving and keep your mouth shut," said Crozier, furious at the Farm Instructor for involving him in what was turning out to be a tactical disaster. "We'll talk with the chiefs. Jefferson, you can interpret."

The mob crowded the four men forward and they had no choice but to move toward the lodge of the chiefs, where in fact, they were being taken.

They ducked through the black oval opening of the lodge, the sudden movement from daylight to the darkness within blinding. As if through an immense distance, Poundmaker stared across the lodge at the four white men, intruders, out of time, out of place. "If you had wished to come to our Thirst Dance, we would have welcomed you as guests. But this is no way to be, bursting in on us."

Big Bear crouched in the dim light cast from the glowing coals and Sleigh saw for the first time the Cree leader who refused a reservation. He leaned forward, his back hunched and misshapen, his face scarred and pitted by smallpox.

Jefferson said, "The police want you to give up the two men Craig says attacked him. It is a small thing, not as serious as you think. All of you may come to see they get a fair trial."

"You must leave this place at once," said Big Bear. "We cannot speak of this matter until the Thirst Dance is over."

Jefferson hastily translated for Crozier, though there was no need. The message was unmistakably clear.

"Very well," said Crozier. "Tell them, Jefferson, I will hold off until the Thirst Dance ends and only until then. When it ends, I want those men."

Big Bear stepped forward as the four white men backed out of the lodge. "We will come down to the Instructor's house," he said. "You may take your prisoners there." And then, almost as an afterthought, hinted at the trouble to come. "If you can."

Outside, Crozier's mind reeled in the heat. His eyes scanned the hills. He sensed forces gathering and recognized the serious difficulty he was in. A plan, he had to have a plan. But all he could think of was to muster every available man from the barracks in Battleford. He mounted and rode out of the Cree camp, the incessant drumming and chanting reminding him of his failure to make an arrest. His armoured breast-plate began to work itself loose, the gait of the horse causing it to chafe at his chest.

In the Thirst Dance lodge, unrecognized by Craig, the two men danced on. The whole camp knew they were there. The Clothes and Man Who Speaks Our Language had made fools, first of Craig, now the police. They danced and weaved, glancing over the barrier that separated them from the women, reaching for some fragment from the warrior's past.

Moving in their soft smoke-tanned dresses, their hair shining and plaited, the young women passed them in the dance, turning their dark brown eyes away from the two men. They would not look upon them as their mothers had once favoured Fine Day when he returned in victory from his raid on the Sioux many years ago. For it was not as before and never would be again. The Clothes and Man Who Speaks Our Language had brought the police into the holy place.

THE WOMEN ON THE BRIDGE

Battleford, November, 1884

As the Gowanlocks' buckboard approaches the bridge below Battleford, Indian women converge on the wagon and prevent their crossing.

Theresa Gowanlock's husband of two weeks talks to them in Cree. Twenty-eight years old and beginning to bald, John Gowanlock has a thin face and the harried look of a man seeking his fortune in the North-West. He explains they are on the last leg of a long journey, have no supplies left and nothing to give them. Theresa doesn't understand Cree, but sitting beside her husband on the buckboard and looking into the weathered brown faces of the women, she senses he is telling them this.

There are seven women and a dog pulling a small travois, poles crossed on its harnessed shoulders. They surround her with their foreign presence, their eyes touching each detail of her clothing, until finally, stripped naked, it is *she* who is foreign, one of the only white women in the Territory.

She cannot possibly know what the small bundles piled on the travois contain, only that whatever is within them may be the sum of their worldly possessions. Still, beneath the blankets they wrap themselves in, they are, like her, women. She wonders how they live, how they survive, and how they have come to be here on the bridge.

They must have been hidden by the poplar trees that line the far side of the riverbank. The Gowanlocks have arrived in late fall and ice is already forming at the river's edge. It breaks off in shards that swirl downriver. Beyond the bridge she sees a few squat buildings.

"Our welcoming committee," says her husband and flicks the reins. The horses jerk the buckboard into motion as the women quickly move aside. "Welcome to Battleford, my dear!" he shouts. "Formerly the capital of the North-West Territories." Is it irony, anger, or both, that she hears in his voice?

Her husband urges the horses forward as she turns to look back at the small ragged band of women who hold her vision even as they recede from it.

"I want you to wait in town until the house is finished," he tells her.

She cannot believe he would leave her in such a desolate God-forsaken place as Battleford. "Let me go with you," she begs.

"I want everything to be ready, the house perfect for you. Stay here with the Lauries. I'll go on to Frog Lake and send for you when the house is ready. It won't be more than a month. I promise."

Patrick Laurie's brother, Richard, is John Gowanlock's partner in the Frog Lake enterprise. Patrick Laurie is also the writer, editor, publisher, and printer of a one-man newspaper, *The Saskatchewan Herald*. Like everything else in Battleford the *Herald* was founded on the premise that Battleford would remain the capital of the North-West and on the route of the proposed railway.

Laurie stands in frozen mud in the middle of nowhere in front of a ramshackle structure surrounded by a bastion of upright and askew fence posts he calls his editorial office. "What a little sheet!" he proclaims, proudly waving a page proof at her.

Humouring him, Theresa nods her head enthusiastically. Privately she thinks him quite mad. Since she has been staying with the Lauries, she has learned a great deal about Laurie, and by reading his newspaper, a great deal about the region.

Patrick Gammie Laurie fancies himself an advance guard of settlement sending word from the outer edge of the frontier back to a more civilized world. "That great Canadian journalistic pioneer," the *Hamilton Spectator* calls Laurie, who reprints this description of himself in the pages of his own paper.

When Theresa isn't helping Laurie's wife, Effie, with chores, she reads back issues of his newspaper, anxious to understand where she is. For the first time she learns of the four-day confrontation between the police and the combined war parties of Big Bear and Poundmaker that very summer. Why hasn't her husband told her about this? The newspaper is full of it. What is he hiding? Why has he gone ahead without her?

She discovers it then, the announcement of her wedding and as she reads it sees her marriage in an alarming new light.

MARRIED

GOWANLOCK — JOHNSON.

On Wednesday, October 1st, at the residence of the bride's father, by the Rev. Wardner, John A. Gowanlock, of Battleford, Saskatchewan Territory, to Miss Theresa M., daughter of Mr. H. Johnson, of Tintern, Lincoln Co., Ont.

J.A. Gowanlock, who went east some weeks ago to purchase machinery for a grist and saw mill to be put up at Frog Lake by himself and R.C. Laurie, returned on Friday last, and on his arrival here found the gratifying intelligence awaiting him that the machinery had arrived at Swift Current. It is intended to put in two run of stones, but for the present they will only bring one run and a forty-four-inch saw.

> The building will be ready for the
> machinery by the time it arrives.
> Mr. Gowanlock has closed his store here
> and will go out to the lake next week.
> While down east he took unto himself
> one of Ontario's fair daughters and
> brought her out west to grow up with the
> country.

She scans the two paragraphs in the newspaper to see
where the part about her marriage ends and the part about
the mill machinery begins, but it is all one piece.

"Tacked on the end like some afterthought," she sighs, as
the six-week stale news falls to her bed.

What a fool she'd been to allow this to happen to her. At
first it had seemed so romantic, an adventure. Her betrothed,
a young man from Parkdale, Ontario, had gone west seeking
his fortune. Had he not strategically placed himself at what
promised to be the gateway to the Territory, the hub of
commercial activity and capital of the North-West Territories,
Battleford? It seemed so. And at what point did she first realize
that all was not as it seemed?

She does not confront these disturbing thoughts directly,
but rather, obliquely. They nag at the corners of her mind and
when they become too disquieting, too real, she dismisses
them.

"A place for everything and everything in its place," her
mother would say. She hates not having her own place. It
heightens her disorientation, her sense of being alone in an
unknown country. She tells herself she will feel better when

her things arrive and she unpacks them. She longs to surround herself with familiar tangibles.

Six weeks he's left her waiting in Battleford while he's up
at Frog Lake with thirteen men working on the dam, the mill,
the house, left her waiting like a piece of machinery for his
mill.

She wraps herself in a shawl, then realizes this will not be
enough and puts on her coat. She shuts the door, and steps
outside. A plain-looking woman, she wears her dark hair
parted in the middle and tied in a bun. Against the advice of
the Lauries, she has taken to walking about the town alone.
In the intervening six weeks of waiting for her husband's
return, fall has turned to winter and second thoughts about
her marriage to serious misgivings.

She is walking in the new upper town just then being built
and to which people are moving from the flats on the south
side of the Battle River where it floods each spring. By
relocating on higher land between the Battle and
Saskatchewan Rivers, residents hope to escape the hazards of
floods, and by being next to the Mounted Police barracks, the
increasing resentment of the thousands of Crees that surround them.

As she makes her way beyond the single street and stands
looking into the valley below, she feels utterly and completely
alone, abandoned, like one of the empty shacks on the
Battleford River flats: skinny logs that lie length-wise no
higher than the reach of the man who put them there, a cotton
sack for a window, a piece of raw-hide hanging from a door
frame.

"Men," her mother warned her, "when left to their own devices, most certainly run amok in the worst possible ways. But you'll see plenty of that where you're going. That's why they need us, to civilize them."

Now that the town is moving to higher ground it exists in two different places, but because of the split in opinion over the location of the townsite, fully and finally in neither, a town that can't make up its mind. Like some men. Like her husband.

Her eyes follow the cold green river coiling and uncoiling through the bare trees. She searches the valley below, wondering what is across the bridge, on the other side, the wilderness that claims her husband and from which he will soon return to take her to Frog Lake.

Though she does not see it at first, her mind filled with concern for herself and her husband, a stray horse stands on the bridge Theresa Gowanlock stares down upon from the height of the hill. The horse has caught a rear hoof between the timbers and is trapped, its fate already sealed. She sees it now. It paws the air in panic, then collapses in exhaustion. The mare lies on its side gathering strength, for surely, she recognizes this in its vulnerability, it is a mare.

From the far side of the river, three Indian women begin walking toward the bridge. As they approach it and begin to walk across, she is reassured that they will know what to do about the unfortunate horse now heaving on its side.

The three women bend over the horse and she glimpses the flash of their knives as they fall upon the mare.

With its scaffolding and plank deck, the bridge is like a wooden stage suspended above the bottom of the valley. She is held, fascinated, unable to avert her eyes from the scene unfolding below.

While the women work with their knives, the horse's legs thrash in short spasmodic twitches. One of the women folds the slippery hide while the other two carve the carcass into pieces they can carry. They hurl away the hooves and the head, and fling the intestines in an arc that ends with a splash in the water below. There are other women on the bridge now. They carry off a half-haunch and disappear through the trees. Others follow, carrying huge chunks of the horse. Theresa Gowanlock stares down on the butchering below, unable to believe it is happening, unable to stop watching.

In less than twenty minutes all evidence of the horse and the women is gone and it is possible to believe for just a moment that she did not see the slaughter, that it didn't happen. She has mistakenly opened the door to the wrong room and has seen something she shouldn't have seen. Now she tries to shut it. On the bridge between settlement and wilderness, she has glimpsed a part of the country she had not known existed, where the only law is the reality dictated by the moment. But the door in her mind will not stay shut. She does not think of them first as Indians or savages, but as women. She tries to imagine their circumstances, but she can't. She can't begin to.

And where were their men? She hadn't seen a single man. When she returns to the Laurie's house she asks Effie about them.

"If you mean that heathen bunch what whoop and beat the drum all day long in front of Sandy Macdonald's store disturbin' decent Christians with their infernal beggin' dance, they's gone back to Frog Lake and that's not near far enough away for me. Why can't they get themselves onto a reservation where they belong?"

Theresa Gowanlock hasn't been in the country long enough to develop such firm convictions about these matters, but she listens to the woman's loud bitterness with considerable alarm. "You mean to say," she asks, "they don't have a reservation?"

"This bunch never signed no treaty," replies the woman. "This used to be a decent place till the government got it into their heads we didn't need a railroad and Battleford wasn't the capital of the Northwest anymore. And what do we get instead? Why we get the Indians. It's their fault. Them and that damn Dewdney!"

Since the disquieting scene on the bridge nothing seems certain. The capital is not the capital, the town is moving to a new site, Big Bear's band has not settled on a reserve. She is married but without her husband.

She believes that in essential matters of business the men know what they are doing. The mill at Frog Lake, the cutting of lumber, the dealings with the Indians, these things the men control and do well.

She clings to the belief that once she arrives at Frog Lake and surrounds herself with familiar objects in her own house, she will learn to feel at home in this alien land. She must, for it is all she has left. She envisions her new home as the place of her happiness, a foundation of stability in a wilderness of flux and change, and longs for her husband to come and take her there.

"I thought I'd go mad," she breathes. "Promise you'll never leave me like this again, John." Secure in his arms, her head against his chest, she does not tell him what she has seen and learned in his absence.

The next morning they load their wagon with supplies and begin their final journey to the distant outpost of Frog Lake. Tools, sacks of flour and salted pork give the wagon a weight that carries it with gathering momentum into the bottom of the river valley where, before she can prepare for it, the bridge looms before her.

The actual clop-clop of the horses' hooves hit the timbers first, then the wagon itself. Now she sees it all again, not from the distance of the hill, but so close it is as if she is actually there with the women at the butchering, each detail magnified over and over in her mind: the arc of the animal's steaming guts flung from the bridge unfurl in the cold winter air over the river, tearing something loose within her until all she can do is scream and scream again as her husband stands in the buckboard, both arms reining the horses to a halt.

In the stillness of the stopped wagon and the warmth of his embrace, she closes her eyes and feels herself suspended somewhere between the life she left in Ontario and the place her husband is taking her. She opens them again and glimpses, between gaps in the planking, jagged chunks of ice on the cold swift current. And there, soaked into the boards by rain, beneath the thin clear sheet of ice forming on the planks, the blood of the horse.

"Please, let's not stop here," she says.

And her worried husband, helpless to understand any of this, can do nothing now but drive the horses on.

The wagon trundles across the bridge with a clatter, gains the other side, climbs the steep incline and disappears into the trees.

DINNER AT FORT PITT

Fort Pitt, December, 1885

"To keep the animals in," John Gowanlock says as they walk through the unguarded front gate of the fence that surrounds the rough-hewn, spruce log structures inside.

He means livestock, she knows, staring up at the steep-pitched rooftops, thinking that since arriving in the North-West she has seen behaviour that certainly could lead her to believe otherwise, her gaze dropping to the snow-bound yard where her growing disbelief in the difference between men and animals is further confirmed.

Four men examine a fur, pulling and tugging at the pelt.

"Red fox," enthuses her husband. "This is the season."

She feels the hard look of a lean, blond young man, barely twenty, who has already been places she hopes she will never go. Passing close to the crew of men who tug at the four points of the pelt, she avoids his eyes, first by looking down at the fur, each hair of the fox tipped with white and silver-grey, then glancing up at the building her husband guides her toward.

It is the main building, the one most resembling a dwelling where people might live, though she can't imagine who. Small blank second-storey windows stare down at her trapped in her husband's world. Closer, she watches the black iron handle turn in the arched timber door and imagines the people on the other side: traders and unseemly adventurers who smell bad and act worse. But the door opens instead on a woman wiping her hands on an apron, stepping forward, embracing her.

"I'm Helen McLean! I've heard so much about you from John, but he's kept you hiding in Battleford forever and now . . ." the McLean woman steps back, touching her lightly on the shoulders and looking into her face, "and now, here you are at last! Welcome to Fort Pitt!"

"And yes," she thinks, "but where exactly is Fort Pitt, and where, exactly, am I?"

"Poor dear!" the McLean woman says. "You must be tired from your journey. The girls will show you to your room. Girls!" she calls into the hallway. "Come and meet our guest.

"A little rest before dinner and you'll be good as new! We've asked a few friends to join us, nothing formal. Just some people in the area I know you'll want to meet. Eliza! Kitty! Come take Mrs. Gowanlock to her room!"

One of the girls takes her arm and guides her up the narrow wooden stairway. "I'm Elizabeth." Ahead, a tall girl with dark braids bounds up the steps two at a time. "That's Katherine."

The girls place her bags on a rug spread over the wide planked floor of a second-storey room and stare as if she is a curiosity from another world. "We're so glad you've come," bursts Elizabeth, breaking the shy silence of the room. "You must tell us everything. About your trip. What it's like in the East."

They stand on either side of her, each beginning a statement the other finishes, sisters so close they seem two halves of one person. "Just everything!" repeats Katherine.

But before she can speak a single word, Elizabeth changes the subject and says, "Kitty and I planned the setting so we can sit on either side of you at the table. We put Duncan next to Inspector Dickens. You'll see. It's perfect!"

"Mother says you must rest before dinner so we'll have to wait till then," Katherine quickly adds.

"In the meantime," offers Elizabeth, pointing at something Katherine holds, "you may find this a pleasant surprise."

Katherine passes it to her: a puzzle. She turns the tapered, hollow, cone-shaped object in her hands; fragments and pieces of something loose tumble inside.

"Look through the hole in the tapered end," urges Katherine. "Go ahead, try it."

She presses the mahogany cone to her eye and squints through a peep-hole into a world of translucent coloured glass. "This is so beautiful," forgetting for a moment where she is.

Tiny pieces of coloured glass rearrange themselves and tumble into a pattern of perfectly symmetrical six-fold illumination; endlessly changing, never repeated, one small turn of the cone and the snowflakes of coloured glass fall irrevocably into a new pattern.

"It's a kaleidoscope. Father got it for us," says Katherine as the sisters back toward the door on tip-toe. "It's all the fashion in London. It's done with mirrors."

The McLean sisters slip through the door, then pull their heads around to peer in and say, "We're going to help mother get ready now. Try to sleep. We'll wake you in time."

She enters a long dining hall aglow in candlelight reflected off silver that illuminates the faces of dinner guests watching the self-conscious newcomer take her place. As William McLean guides her to the table she thinks this: last night I stayed at a half-breed's house and drank tea made in the same water the potatoes were boiled in; tonight I am being escorted to dinner on the arm of the factor of Fort Pitt — a perspective to focus on while trying not to be overwhelmed by the grand formality of the dinner setting and the dress of the guests.

"We've put you with the girls, Mrs. Gowanlock," her host says from behind, moving her chair. "I'll sit with your husband."

John is counting on her to make a good impression. It is essential to his business. A government contract to build a mill at Frog Lake. Trading with the Indians. Land and timber deals. The truth is she has been married two months to a man moving fast on the far edge of the frontier, a man who combined their honeymoon with a trip east to buy machinery and then left her waiting six weeks in Battleford.

But at last, here are the girls! How beautiful they look, changed now from the plain dark woollen house dresses of this afternoon to forest-green velvet and garnet satin. An unusual necklace made of thin cylinders of bone strung together with large brass beads moves against Katherine's dress.

How do they manage, cut off from the civilized world, to dress in the height of fashion from the pages of *The Young Ladies Journal* or *The Queen*? But their father is the factor of a Hudson's Bay post and she mustn't stare or let on that this Sunday dinner is different from any other Sunday of her life.

"Duncan will say grace," announces the father from the far end of the table.

"Dear Lord," intones Duncan.

A raised turquoise border encircles a painting by William Bartlett of the Chaudière Bridge in the centre of the plate set before her bowed head. Duncan is still saying grace and no one will notice she hasn't closed her eyes. How peaceful the bridge is, so different from the one at Battleford where the Indian women ... but she won't think of that, not now, cherishing instead the idyllic scene painted on her plate, and she cannot help herself, now while the others have their heads bowed, their eyes closed, she must, she will touch it. The tips of her fingers move over the raised floral pattern of the turquoise border as she drifts with two small sail-boats painted on a mirrored surface of porcelain, and then the moment shatters, sudden and sure as if the plate itself has shattered in her hands — someone is watching her. But who? She is afraid to look up but knows she must. How embarrassing!

It is Elizabeth, her conspiratorial smile telling her the secret of the plate is safe. The sisters have been watching throughout grace, carrying on a silent conversation of grimaces, meaningful glances, and barely suppressed laughter.

These girls — a distraction and pure mischief. She must ignore them and concentrate instead on sinking her fork into a slice of lamb while her husband talks to McLean about the mill at Frog Lake and the house he has built.

"Of course, there's some inside finishing work still to be done."

She listens, intent for tangible details to help her envision the new home she will see for the first time two days' journey from tonight.

"You see," her husband speaks to the Hudson's Bay factor with an earnest intensity reserved for those he thinks important enough to advance his station in life, "a grand opportunity is opening to trade with the Indians up there. I want to put in some trade goods and a small store on the main floor of the house."

Two months' journeying to her home, and before she gets there, her husband has built a trading post in it. Worse, she learns of it second-hand, listening in on a conversation. He insists on keeping things from her, business matters she is not privy to and yet to which, as his wife, her fate is inextricably bound. He leads a life quite separate from her. She feels betrayed, cheated, alone.

"Aren't you rushing into things too quickly with this mill of yours?" asks McLean.

"That may be true," counters her husband, "though I doubt the government would put the building of the mill out for tender if they didn't see a future for the area."

"What's the point of building a flour mill up there when the Indians haven't even settled on a reserve, much less planted any wheat?" asks McLean.

"Ah," sighs the military man with the bright red beard who sits next to Katherine's brother Duncan, "the Indians." He must be the Inspector Dickens the girls spoke of. He seems to be talking to himself, for no one is listening but her, unnoticed. "Frankly, I would have preferred the Cape. I have always had a fondness for elephants. But here I am in Canada, part of a police force protecting the western aborigine from whiskey traders."

He seems to shuffle through fragments of his life as he puzzles over his plight, a process she herself has become familiar with of late; like composing letters that explain where you are but having no one to send them to.

"Hiring me to thwart whiskey traders was rather like setting the fox to guard the chicken house," he says, staring straight ahead. "What would father think, if he could see me now?" Then, as if to share some confidence with her, he leans across the table and she too leans forward, straining to hear him.

"Stuck in the Canadian mud!" He slumps forward in his chair and his head bobs into a sleeping nod as he withdraws into mutterings that to him alone make sense.

"There's government for you, Gowanlock," says McLean. "I'm afraid Inspector Dickens is the only government up here and he had one leg in the bag long before dinner began. I've made my views known, but as you can see he is often not with us. No, the government doesn't give a damn about us and that's precisely why I worry about you and your mill at Frog Lake."

"Surely you aren't suggesting..." begins her husband.

"This fall the tension was terrible. The government ordered Indian agents to cut down on rations, and even then, to issue them only to those on reservations. Big Bear hasn't complied and his people are starving. He often comes to the fort, searching for what he cannot find. He wants only a fair deal and can't get one, so instead, he wanders the countryside, an old man asking questions no one can answer. Reminds me a bit of Lear, don't you see?" McLean pauses, wiping the corner of his mouth with a napkin. "A dethroned monarch wandering the countryside. And like Lear, the offspring have turned on their father. And there are others. Wandering Spirit is being drawn into their circle. Little Poplar has come all the way from Montana to be a part of this."

"A part of what?" asks her husband.

"Aren't you forgetting something?" Helen McLean interrupts.

"I don't think so. I thought it a rather good analogy."

"Except for one important difference. Lear's *daughters* turned on him, but in the case of Big Bear it is his son." The McLean woman looks directly at her husband. "It is the *men*, not the women, who spoil things here, and quite frankly, I think you're spoiling our dinner! I'm sure our young bride from Ontario doesn't care to hear of such matters, having only just arrived. Do you, my dear?"

Everyone is waiting for her reply, but she can't think of what to say. She only knows she keeps hearing of Big Bear and his band of Plains Cree who have not settled on a reservation, and that her husband plans to trade with these same Indians *out of their house.* Her hand shakes so badly she sets her fork down on the table-cloth.

McLean balls a napkin in his closed hands.

A very old man with a brown weathered face and a snow-white beard bends over the table and places a dish on it. In the silence he seems to take forever.

McLean's crumpled napkin falls to the table. "I'm afraid you've outdone yourself tonight," he tells the old man in a cheerful tone, as if the ominous discussion had never taken place.

The old man must be the cook and at last she sees her opening. "Yes," she says in a pleasant, almost trance-like voice, "the lamb was quite lovely."

One of Katherine and Elizabeth's younger sisters rolls her eyes in amusement. "It's not lamb, it's beaver! Kitty, why don't *you* tell Mrs. Gowanlock about our Indians."

"Yes, do," urges Duncan. "You must, you know."

"Sitting Bull traded six ponies for these beads and gave them to me before he left the country." Katherine holds them out from her dress for her to see. "It's because I'm such a good shot. Besides, I was his favourite."

If she were their age she too might see this as an adventure, instead of feeling fear for herself and her husband.

"Really girls!" Helen McLean rushes from the kitchen to scold her daughters. "What will our guest think if you carry on this way? Please, take Mrs. Gowanlock to the parlour where we can rest and leave these men to themselves.

"I know how you must feel," she says, "coming here like this in the dead of winter. But wait until spring when you can listen to the wind in the poplars and watch it comb through the grass. I have lived in this country all my life and, like my husband, my father was a Hudson's Bay factor. There is so much I want to show you. Look at these girls. They love their life here. Born and raised in the country, like their mother."

"It *was* a lovely dinner," Theresa says.

"Our cook, Otto Dufresne, deserves the credit. He knows the country so well. How to get the most out of it. That's the key out here. To adapt."

"You seem to have adapted very well," she hears herself say.

Within the walls of the fort the McLeans have created their own inner world of family. Can she too dare to dream of having her own children, of raising a family in this wilderness?

"Come and see," says Helen McLean. "We have the only organ in the West just waiting in the parlour to be played."

"Do you know 'The Lost Chord'?" asks Elizabeth.

"It's our favourite," says Katherine. "You must join us."

The girls gather around their mother and Duncan follows his sisters, leaving only her husband, McLean, and the military man, Inspector Dickens, now unsuccessfully attempting to rise from the dinner table.

"I have already had the pleasure of hearing 'The Lost Chord' sung by the McLeans." He grasps the back of his chair for support. "Believe me when I say, Mrs. Gowanlock, once you have heard their unique rendition, the word *lost* will take on new meaning." He lurches from his chair and weaves down the hallway.

"I'm afraid it's our Inspector who is lost," Duncan says. "But never mind all that, Mother's setting up in the parlour."

Ranging in age from Elizabeth and Katherine to the small girl in the chocolate brown dress who peers at her through bangs, the McLean children sit in the parlour in a circle around their mother, waiting for her to join them.

"I only play it when we have company," Helen McLean says, seated at her great pride.

Ignoring their mother, the McLean children attempt to outdo each other telling tales of their experiences with the Indians. Duncan claims to have been adopted by a band of Saulteaux at birth, while Kitty says Sitting Bull made her an Indian princess.

"Have you met Charles Dickens' son?" asks Duncan, realizing he can't top his sister with Indian stories.

"Of course not," she replies. The abruptness of her answer reflects the impatience of a full day spent travelling across the country, the dinner, unravelling now into a nonsensical riddle. Confused, she wonders aloud, "How could I?"

"He lives right here in the fort," Duncan says. "I thought I saw him talking to you at the table, but perhaps he was talking to himself. He often does, you know."

"Lives here in the fort?" she hears herself say, and at this precise moment senses something happening to her. She is becoming one of the children, for they have drawn her into their circle. "Lives in the fort?" she repeats. "Who lives in the fort?"

"In the barracks," Duncan says. "Next time you're here, we'll visit. Inspector Dickens is in charge of our Mounted Police. Imagine. Our defence, if it should ever come to that, but of course, it won't, would be in the hands of the son of a famous novelist. Wouldn't that be an adventure?"

"Yes. Imagine," she says. "Imagine that!" But she cannot and will not imagine such a thing.

Hands poised, their mother looks down from the organ, signals she is ready. With a nod to the girls, she strikes the keys, and over the rich sonorous sound of the organ float the words to "The Lost Chord."

> *It quieted pain and sorrow,*
> *Like love overcoming strife.*
> *It seemed the harmonious echo*
> *From our discordant life.*
> *It linked all perplexed meanings*
> *Into one perfect piece,*
> *And trembled away into silence*
> *As if it were loath to cease.*

In the circle of children she no longer feels alone. The music is having a quite different effect on her than that predicted by the bitter lonely man who spoke to her at the dinner table. Inspector Dickens. Imagine. Charles Dickens' son.

She sits on the floor holding hands with Katherine and Elizabeth and for the first time in months feels outside herself and her fears as, swept up in the song and the power of the organ, she joins in the singing:

> *I have sought, but I seek in vain,*
> *That one lost chord divine,*
> *Which came from the soul of the organ*
> *And entered into mine.*

Something is wrong; not the song, not the melody, but the words. Without warning, in mid-verse, the girls have abruptly switched to Cree and she is no longer able to sing with them.

Is this what Inspector Dickens meant by a unique rendition that would give new meaning to the word *lost?* If so, then it is the cruellest of jokes, for though the Cree sung by the McLean girls has a pleasant enough musical quality it is completely foreign to her and quite suddenly it is she who is lost.

She is not part of the McLeans or the life they lead at Fort Pitt and never can be. Separate and shut off from the real world, clothed in the latest fashion, waited on by servants, Helen McLean and her children live an extravagant illusion. The walls of Fort Pitt are blinders behind which the McLeans maintain a myopic denial of who and where they are: a handful of whites in an unknown land surrounded by thousands of starving Indians.

The song in Cree cannot include her. An immense tired-
ness is enveloping and overwhelming her. The room turns like
the girls' kaleidoscope, Katherine's and Elizabeth's upraised
alarmed faces swirling into a blur as she falls into darkness.

She sits up in bed. What hour is it? Where is her husband?
She doesn't know, only that it is night. She stares open-eyed
into the darkness of a room filled with fragments of a dream
so frightening it has just wakened her: a horse trapped on the
Battleford bridge . . . Indian women falling on it with their
knives. In her dream she is on the bridge with the Indian
women; in her dream she has become one of them. She is
living the life of a Cree woman scavenging meat from a
crippled horse caught on the bridge. How different from the
elaborate meal served within the walls of Fort Pitt.

She parts the curtain: a flat expanse of snow illuminated
by moonlight, and beyond the far edge of the field, the river
that runs through her dream and churns under the bridge at
Battleford, the North Saskatchewan.

Something terrible will happen. She feels a powerful
foreboding, certain and irreversible as the river itself, its
winding looping coils defined by the dark hills rising behind
it.

Footsteps on the stairs. Someone is coming. She draws
the curtain. In the darkened room, her husband, a man she
doesn't know, steps quietly toward the bed believing she is
asleep.

SKATING ON THIN ICE

Frog Lake, March 28, 1885

Cameron locked the door behind him and looked into the grey northern sky — just enough light to get to Gowanlock's before nightfall if he skated instead of walking.

Striding toward the lake, he thought of the woman who passed him briefly in the yard at Fort Pitt, a pretty thing dragged along on the arm of her strong-willed husband. That was in December. Now it was the end of March, the ice was melting, and they had invited him for dinner.

Cameron walked toward the lake, his casual gait belying any fear he might feel as one of a small group of whites surrounded by Crees in this isolated settlement. As a trader, he knew that to gain their respect and friendship he must never show he was afraid. He wasn't always successful.

Cameron knelt at the lake's edge and looked into the film of water on the thawing ice at his reflection: the thin angular face of a young man who had survived a winter living alone in the wilderness. He bent to study it further and saw, mirrored in the reflection of the poplars, the barely discernible movement of a rider through the trees.

He did not turn to acknowledge the rider, seen only by chance, but instead trailed his fingers through the film of water, at once touching and dispelling the reflection. The Indians were everywhere a presence, and like the land, a mirror in which each man might find himself.

Even though he had no idea of ice conditions two miles down the creek where the young couple were building their mill, Cameron decided the ice on the lake would hold and resolved to skate to Gowanlock's for dinner. He sat on a log and strapped the blades to his boots. Then Cameron hobbled onto the wet ice and with a downward thrust of an angled blade glided in a wide arcing turn toward the south end of the lake. Searching the shore he no longer saw the Indian, but sighting the break in the trees that marked the mouth of the creek, he began skating toward it. In the rhythmic steady nicking slash of his skate blades, his thoughts streamed through the rush of the coming night as he remembered how he first came here.

... *just a kid then and believing every word when cousin Joe Woods gave him a fire-bag he said belonged to a Sioux named Rain-in-the-Face when Joe was stationed with the Mounted Police at Fort Walsh.*

"The coals of hell are in that fire-bag, and son, you play with fire, you'll get burned!" Not his father, long dead from a logging accident, but his grandfather, Bleasdell, warning

him the day he almost burned the house down when he
finally got the spark from the flint to catch.

*Magic it was, filled with the wild smell of smoke-tanned
leather and places he wanted to go. Suddenly his
grandfather's stone vicarage and the shade trees that lined
the streets of Trenton seemed tame and civilized.*

*He would go further west than his cousin, thousands of
miles beyond Fort Walsh, where the western edge of the
plains unroll into foothills, and lodge-pole pine and spruce
climb the ragged looming wall of the Rockies. In the mountains, working on the railway until the summer of '84, he
earned a stake for a trading outfit at Pincher Creek: eleven
horses, blankets, traps, ammunition, bacon, tea, cloth, mirrors women can seen themselves in, Perry Davis Pain Killer
for the men.*

*"The frontier," cousin Joe told him, handing him the
fire-bag. "So many buffalo you can't imagine."*

*But the buffalo were just bones. No matter where he went
the best part of the country had vanished before he got to it
— elusive, unreachable, always moving just ahead of him, a
place in his heart he would never arrive at, the frontier.*

*Battleford had become too white and everyone in the
south was waiting for the railway to freight them the same
civilization he was trying to escape. So he headed north until
he reached the last of the free Indians, a band of renegade
Cree without treaty or reservation, wintering on the shore
of the lake on which he now skated.*

He didn't find his uncle's frontier, but he had certainly found the Indians. Surely it was more than coincidence, his being here. Some destiny or design had drawn him to them. Like himself they too were searching for their freedom, refusing to take treaty.

After he and Poundmaker's son broke trail south of Battleford through the Eagle Hills and on to Swift Current, the Cree called him Little Brother. He was twenty-two years old and some shared kinship of spirit prompted them to call him Little Brother...

His thoughts drifted in a free and unconscious reverie as he glided over the ice. He would never go back. Not like his cousin Joe, returning to Ontario. Until the day he died he would move always on the edge of things, an outsider, like these Indians.

The lone figure left the lake, moved into the narrowing mouth of the creek, and vanished among the trees. In the last lingering light of March 28, 1885, William Bleasdell Cameron skated slowly and carefully onto the six-foot-wide ribbon of ice that wound through the poplars, birch, and spruce, colder now, and darker, on the creek.

Unlike the freedom of the open lake where he hadn't noticed the ice water thrown up by his skate blades splattering his thick wool pants to the knees, here, in the close confines of the creek, he felt the heavy weight of the water freezing in the falling temperature. The shock of frozen stiff wool on his legs shuddered through him. Cameron stopped on the creek ice in the fading light and chill air and considered his folly. A log laden with snow slanted across the creek, blocking his way. He could easily climb over but then what? An unexpected combining of circumstances — a sudden drop in temperature, melting ice refreezing — and he was completely at the mercy of the elements.

He would never make it to Gowanlock's now. He had to get off the ice and keep moving toward the shelter and warmth of Big Bear's camp. He pulled his flannel-lined mitts off and unstrapped the blades from his boots, though not quickly enough, for when he replaced his mitts, his thumbs were numb. His boots crunched through the ice-glazed crust of snow that bordered the creek as he searched for the trail. Already he was losing feeling in his feet as he moved along the compacted snow of the trail that led back to the settlement through Big Bear's camp.

Finally, the smoke and smell of the Indian camp. Cameron staggered forward into startled Cree voices and snapping dogs and moved between tipis toward the main lodge. He dropped to his knees, lifted the lodge flap, and quickly crawled through the oval opening into the darkness inside.

Surprised, the men shifted their places in the circle to make room for him. Cameron gratefully placed his hands, palms out, toward the small fire. Warmth from the burning embers seeped into his body and as the cold dissipated in subsiding waves of pain, he glanced around the dark, smoke-filled tipi for faces familiar from trading at the Hudson's Bay store, the unmistakable and curiously wavy black hair of Wandering Spirit, and the broad defiant face of Big Bear's son, Imasees. But the others were not from Big Bear's tribe, nor was Big Bear himself here, he realized, becoming aware of the silence since he entered the tipi. He was overcome with an awkward sense that he had interrupted something.

The Indians stared into the fire, their dark faces tense, absorbed, and though the silence lasted only a moment, to Cameron it seemed to hang forever in the closeness of the tipi.

The men passed the stone pipe and began to speak in a guarded Cree completely different from the Pidgin-Cree they spoke for Cameron's benefit in the Hudson's Bay store. Ignoring him, they talked among themselves, excluding Cameron as completely as if he didn't exist. He was not connected to them, felt completely alone, and knew now he had interrupted a meeting at which he was not welcome, his presence scarcely acknowledged. Even though his clothes were not yet dry, Cameron's pride told him to leave.

He had thought he knew them, but he only knew that part which they had chosen to reveal, allowing him to think he was on familiar terms for their benefit, a façade of friendly banter across the counter of the Bay store for the young clerk when they wanted something. He had assumed he was in control, but it was *they* who were in control. Cold, calculating, they could manipulate him or turn on him as suddenly as the weather.

The rush of spring air that had swept him onto the ice had vanished in the raw north wind that whipped at the leafless limbs of the poplars.

"I am not lost," he told himself, his voice barely audible in the wind.

Light from a low rising quarter-moon reflected off the glazed snow crust and cast the poplars ahead in black silhouettes. Icy branches cracked in the wind and seemed to palpably scrape the cold air.

He thrust his mittened hands out to shield his eyes and face from the flicking lash of branches as he lunged through the forest, the meaning of his unexpected reception in the Indian camp turning over and over in his mind. He had been searching for the romance of an adolescent adventure. It was the myth of the West that had lured him, not its harsh reality. He was a romantic who had never known where he was until tonight.

As he pushed aside branches a twig caught between the thumb and body of his mitten broke off and was held in his mittened hand. Half mad with cold, clutching the tiny branch which he waved in the air like some magic wand, William Bleasdell Cameron stumbled out of the trees and into the clearing at the Hudson's Bay store at Frog Lake.

HOLY THURSDAY

Frog Lake, April 2, 1885

"What time is it?"

Theresa Gowanlock is calling from the top of the stairs to a woman who shares her first name, Theresa, Theresa Delaney — an incredible coincidence considering they are the only two white women in the settlement.

"About 4:30," says the Delaney woman. "Judging by the light."

The two women stand in Theresa Delaney's kitchen in the first grey light before the dawn of Thursday, April 2, 1885.

"I hope I'm not disturbing you," apologizes Theresa Gowanlock. "But with all the guns going off and the dancing, I couldn't sleep. And just now I heard voices."

"Imasees and John Pritchard came to tell my husband the Metis have stolen our horses."

The night before last Pritchard had delivered a letter to Theresa Gowanlock and her husband from Agent Quinn advising them that the Metis had defeated Crozier at Duck Lake, and that they should leave their house at the mill and come to the settlement at once. Odd, she thinks, and says, "I wonder about that half-breed interpreter, John Pritchard. He knocks on our door with a letter from Quinn and then he comes to your house carrying messages from Big Bear's son. Who does he work for?"

"Why he works for himself," Theresa Delaney says, "like any interpreter. He may be the only man in the settlement who knows what's going on.

"Still, I don't think we really have anything to worry about. Our Indians have no grievances and no complaints to make," she insists. "They are happy in their home in the wilderness and I consider it a great shame for evil-minded people to instill into their excitable heads the false idea that they are persecuted by the government.

"When I say our Indians, I mean those under my husband's control. I look upon the Indian children as my children and my husband looks upon the men as being under his care. They regard him as their father." She pauses, watching her houseguest take in her words.

Theresa Gowanlock turns over in her mind the phrase first used by the McLeans, now by this woman: "Our Indians."

A staccato of rapid rifle fire scatters her thoughts, a sound she will never get used to, the random unfocussed violence of these sudden bursts of gunfire. A tense expectation fills the air. She hears it in the talk of the men and the demented out-of-control gunfire. She says, "And isn't there the slightest shadow of a doubt in your mind that not the Metis, but the Indians themselves might have taken our horses?"

"Always. Always, my dear. But even if it were true, it would never do to let them think, for even a moment, that we doubt their word.

"It's not that I'm braver than you," continues the Delaney woman. "I'm not. I just won't let them see. Once they see you are afraid, they take advantage. They come in here, right into my own kitchen and sit down and help themselves as if you'd made it all just for them. They are the worst possible freebooters."

There is a soft knock on the back door, barely discernible, as if someone knew that people were downstairs in the kitchen to answer it at this early hour. Theresa Delaney stands in the open doorway while a man talks to her in Cree, but Theresa Gowanlock's view of him is blocked by the Delaney woman's back. She watches the Delaney woman close the door, admiring her confidence but unsure of her judgement.

"That was Big Bear's son," says Theresa Delaney. "He feels sorry the horses have been taken. He and his men are entirely to blame. They danced all night and then fell asleep and it was then that the Metis took the horses. But we shouldn't worry because he, Imasees, King Bird, will personally start looking for the horses as soon as it is light." She says this in a rote monotone, remembering the words, translating them now for the Gowanlock woman.

King Bird. What a beautiful but odd and incongruous name for someone as implacable and stolid as Big Bear's son.

No wonder most people call him by his Cree name, Imasees. "And do you believe him? What did you say?"

"Of course, I believe him. I told him it's almost light so he'd best get on with it."

But Theresa Gowanlock is not so easily reassured. Since she and her husband left their home at the mill and came to the settlement two days ago, the men have been in a continuous small informal meeting and whenever she gets within hearing they quickly change the subject, lapse into amenities about the weather, or worse, into silence; her husband huddled with the others in this, the latest phase of his betrayal. It is a bad sign, she thinks, when men and women do not share confidences. Already Quinn, Delaney, and her husband are discussing the stolen horses.

The Delaney woman leans across the table and in a low confidential voice says, "I have my own private opinions upon the causes of this latest unrest but do not deem it well or proper to express them. There are others besides the halfbreeds and Big Bear and his men connected with this affair. There are many objects to be gained by such means and there is a wheel within a wheel in the North-West troubles.

"But never mind all that. Your hands are shaking! We'll take a brandy with our tea. It's the least we can do while we wait for this disturbance to end."

The Delaney woman stands on a chair and reaches onto a high shelf for a brandy bottle.

"That's a beautiful cupboard."

"Why thank you. Williscraft, the old man working at your husband's mill, made it for me. He has such a way with wood."

"Yes," Theresa Gowanlock hears herself say.

But of course, she knew that, recognized his work, for she has one very similar in her own kitchen, and admiring Theresa Delaney's only makes her realize how much she misses her new home and causes her quite suddenly to confront a terrible truth: she will never see it again, nor the treasured pieces of herself with which she so carefully filled it: the furniture from her mother and father's farm in Ontario, the china and family heirlooms that define who she is. Now there is no past and she has no identity; now there is only the tenuous present of a few articles of clothing she carries on her back.

"It will end, you know," Theresa Delaney is saying. "It always does. It's nothing really. You should have been here last summer. All of Battleford barricaded inside the fort for a week while the Indians faced off against the police and not a thing came of it, except in the end one of them went to jail. This is the same sort of thing. You'll see. Say when."

The Delaney woman pours brandy into Theresa Gowanlock's teacup and waits for her to say "when," but she is thinking of her house and doesn't, so finally the Delaney woman takes a small portion for herself, then stands on the chair to return the bottle to the cupboard. "Best not to leave the bottle on the table," she says. "Or for that matter, anything else you might want for yourself."

"My own house would be nice," says Theresa Gowanlock, standing, when the first wave of brandy hits her. She clutches the corner of the table as if it were the only tangible thing left in the world to hang onto. "We're not like you," she insists, hovering over the Delaney woman who sits silent and amazed. "They are not *our* Indians. We, that is, my husband and I, do not work for the Department of Indian Affairs and we are not tied to these people in any way. No, we came out here on a business venture. How I ever let that man make me believe for even one minute that this was the land of opportunity I will never know.

"*Battleford!* That's all he could talk of. Battleford was supposed to be the capital of the North-West. Battleford was on the railway line. Then, overnight they change the route, Regina's the capital, and Battleford? Instead of the railroad, Battleford gets *your* Indians."

She feels better now that she has vented some of the tension but bad that the Delaney woman has borne the brunt of it. "I have no right. Not after the kindness you've shown me. I'm sorry."

"Don't be sorry, Theresa. There is no need. Not between you and me. Since you came in December I've begun to feel at home here for the first time. My life is no longer a lonely life. Now, more than ever, there are just the two of us. Don't think for a moment these men have the slightest control over things here, because they don't. They as much as admitted so yesterday."

Theresa Gowanlock thinks about her husband's error in judgement in predicting the economics of Battleford and their future. She thinks about her husband and the other men meeting in the Delaney house for two days, grappling with the reality of where they really are. And young Bill Cameron, just back from Big Bear's camp, claims the Indians behave as if they'd never known him; even Quinn, an old hand with the Sioux from the States who works for the Department here, said, "I know these Indians well enough to insist we should all leave the settlement immediately."

Inspector Dickens and his men have already left.

"You are on your own now, I'm afraid." Dickens attempted to impart this with some sobriety as the official notice of the departure of the police, but Theresa Gowanlock detected the demented glee in his announcement, as if for him, things were never right unless they had gone as horribly and irrevocably wrong as his own life. "Keep to your dwellings! It's not safe to be abroad!"

And if this is so, why, against the advice of both Quinn and Dickens, have her husband and the others decided to stay on? Stubborn pride. The need to assert that all is well and that the men are in control, when in fact even she can see that neither is true.

The horses have been stolen. Not that it matters; where would they go with horses? Yet without them their isolation is final, complete; they are cut off from the rest of the world. Big Bear's son has been looking for them. Just thirty minutes have elapsed since he reassured the Delaney woman he would find them and surely he has, for now he has returned.

From her chair where she sits at the kitchen table, she can see Imasees standing at the foot of the stairs looking up at them with his arms crossed, as if waiting for someone or something to descend. Half-way up stand Quinn and Delaney and further up, the fringed leggings of an Indian at the top of the stairs. And then without warning or notice she is suddenly watching, one by one, the wooden stock and blue metal of a Winchester rifle, three revolvers, another rifle, not a Winchester, but her husband's old single-shot Snider, the guns passing down from man to man to Imasees who stands at the bottom of the stairs collecting them.

"Exactly what is going on here?" Theresa Delaney asks her husband.

"Imasees and his men are short of firearms and they need ours to defend us from the Metis."

"For God's sake, man," interrupts Quinn, "let's drop the pretence, at least among ourselves. This thing could turn to soup fast. We are prisoners. They have our guns and they have our horses."

Outside somewhere a door is being smashed in — Dill's store or the police barracks. The looting has begun. She wonders what will be left of her house at the mill. They have given themselves over freely and in good faith to the Indians. They are no longer in control of their own lives. And not once did anyone ask her opinion. At what moment did the men decide, against the advice of the police, of Quinn, against all good sense, to stay on in the settlement?

Perhaps it was Father Fafard arguing that they should stay as a demonstration of faith. Or Theresa Delaney's husband thinking it would be a shame to abandon the government provisions. Hadn't Big Bear given John Delaney a peace pipe and told him he was beloved by all the band?

And at what point did the men realize the truth and decide to keep it from her? It doesn't matter now.

Outside, as each hammer blow of the axe smashes into the splintered door of Dill's store, something inside her is breaking: trust, suspension of disbelief, the veneer of her gullibility, wanting to believe Imasees and his men are protecting them from the Metis, all her hopes and aspirations, shattering one by one, blow by blow. She is on her knees now, stripped of all self-deception, naked in the knowledge she can no longer shut out, quietly crying to herself.

Absorbed in their own talk, the men are silenced by her soft sobbing, the sight of her huddled form cradled in the arms of Theresa Delaney.

She tries to stifle her crying and focus on faces blurred by tears: Big Bear, an anxious worried old man stripped of all power and control over his men; the broad implacable face of his son, Imasees; Wandering Spirit, Little Poplar. They are all here, some twenty Indians watching her, the white woman, the first to break.

One of them leans over to talk to her husband. Now her husband is trying to calm her, but she won't listen. He is saying, "They want you to know that you should not be afraid. They will not harm you."

But it is all lies. The men have already resumed talking. Her husband will deal with her now. Except she won't let him. She is being difficult. There, he says it, this man holding her by the wrists, shaking her, her husband, "Don't be difficult, Theresa."

She doesn't care. She will not be deceived any longer, not by him, not by any of them.

But she must regain control of herself or she will never know what is happening. If she just sits here quietly and watches, she can see Wandering Spirit talking to Quinn, demanding something. Big Bear's war chief shakes his fist at Quinn, poor Quinn, who tried to warn them. Now it is all coming down on him. She listens, trying to make out the words.

"Who is at the head of the whites in this country?" Wandering Spirit demands. "Is it the government, or the Hudson's Bay Company, or who?"

Quinn can only answer with a harsh forced laugh. How little they know of us, she thinks, suddenly realizing the significance of Wandering Spirit's question and of Quinn's bitter laugh.

The toll of the church bell echoes through the small settlement and across Frog Lake — Holy Thursday. This morning it will be John Pritchard's boy, his hands wrapped around the rope, ringing in early morning mass. The day, she realizes, as the church bell clashes with the yells of the Crees pillaging Dill's store, has hardly begun and anything might happen.

"I think you should all go to church and pray," says Wandering Spirit. "But first," he adds as an afterthought, "my men will kill an ox."

"Why yes!" John Delaney jumps up. "That can be arranged."

But Wandering Spirit is merely informing him what his men intend to do, not asking his permission. Delaney no longer has any power or control here. Does anyone, she wonders. It comes to her now why Wandering Spirit's question to Quinn disturbs her. The Indians do not have a plan. They are making this up as they go along, and for her, this is even more frightening.

"Go to the church," Wandering Spirit demands, moving through the house.

"We'd better go with the others," her husband says, as if they have any choice in the matter.

She tightly grasps her husband's hand and begins walking slowly up the hill toward the church, the Delaneys, Quinn, the other whites, and the Indians behind them.

The smell of burning wood fills the air. Dill's store is in flames and the Indians dart in and out of the smoke and move hurriedly between buildings. Amidst the smoke and raucous cries, the steady, strangely out-of-place ringing of the church bell, she moves up the hill, as in a trance.

Wandering Spirit circles the group on horsebackand just as they reach the top of the hill catches sight of Cameron. "Why don't you go to church with your friends?" he shouts, waving his arm toward the others.

She wonders what will happen if Cameron decides to disobey this thinly veiled order, but the young Hudson's Bay clerk quickly joins the procession.

Theresa Gowanlock and her husband move between two armed Indians standing guard on either side of the church door. As they step inside, young Father Marchand, down from Onion Lake to assist in the service, is about to close the door but is stopped by Father Fafard. "Let the doors remain open so those who wish may enter."

Fafard turns and walks down the aisle, toward the altar, his back to the congregation, so that she and everyone else in the church except Fafard himself see Wandering Spirit's silent moccasined feet stalk down the aisle behind the priest who, stooping forward now to don his white vestments, steps to the altar and turns to see, here, in the centre of his church, the upturned, streaked-with-black-war-paint face of Wandering Spirit, his Winchester butt-ended and pointing heavenward, Wandering Spirit kneeling before him, his rifle in his hand.

The small church seethes with the energies of these two men, this conflict between a priest and his congregation of Woods Cree on one side, and on the other, a war chief and his Plains Cree warriors. Standing at the back of the church Theresa Gowanlock hovers on the periphery, on the brink of this clash of opposites that threatens to consume them all.

And at the centre, Father Fafard begins the invocation in Cree, then falters, as the Plains Cree outside whoop and holler and move through the open door strutting and weaving into the church.

"I forbid you to do any harm," Father Fafard tells them. "Go away quietly to your camps and do not disturb the happiness and peace of the community."

Wandering Spirit rises and faces his own men. "Go!" he shouts.

As the Plains Cree shuffle out of the church, they glance back at their leader who waves his rifle at the whites huddled in the rear of the church. "Go to his place," he says, his rifle pointing at John Delaney.

When Theresa Gowanlock and the others come out of the church they are surrounded by armed Indians waiting to escort them back to the Delaneys'. They are almost fifty feet down the hillside when Little Bear, glancing back from his horse, sees Father Fafard silhouetted against the church door, about to close it. He wheels his horse and gallops back to the church. The priest has almost closed the door when Little Bear leaps from his horse, forces the door open and pumps his fist into Father Fafard's eye.

"Hurry and catch up with the others," orders Little Bear.

Hands pressed to his face, the priest staggers forward, a small robed figure stumbling blindly down the hill toward her. This is the end, Theresa Gowanlock thinks, the end of everything.

The Delaney house has become a central gathering place to which the Indians are directing all the whites in the settlement, for what purpose and to what end she cannot imagine or is afraid to think.

Wandering Spirit keeps trying to get information from Quinn. Who is their leader? The Queen? The government? The Hudson's Bay? Who is it? It strikes her again how little knowledge these people have of the world she comes from.

Cameron is ordered to the Bay store to provide the Indians with whatever they request. Father Fafard's eye is already swollen shut. Chief in name only, Big Bear alternately offers reassurance and warning.

"I am afraid," he blurts to John Delaney, "afraid some of my young men will shoot the whites." Then quickly adds, "But don't worry. You will be safe."

No one is in control. Wandering Spirit gives orders, but Imasees is always present. Silent, since the deception of the horses.

For surely it was deception. She senses his hand in things, though in what way she cannot tell.

Perhaps it is the continued pretence that these Cree warriors are protecting them from the half-breeds, an extension of the story of the stolen horses with which Imasees began the morning, that makes her think this. Imasees, standing at the bottom of the stairs collecting the guns. Their guns.

Wandering Spirit wants everyone to go to the Indian camp, but Quinn is arguing with him.

"We will all go to our camp now, so that we can be together and defend you better from the half-breeds."

This is all a lie. But to what end, she wonders.

Quite unexpectedly her husband comes to her. "You had best put your shawl around you for it is very cold," he says, as if they are going for a walk together, but then adds, "Perhaps we will not be gone long."

But he doesn't really know and what he says makes very little sense, though now that she thinks about it, no more and no less than anything else he has ever said.

She has been walking for some time now, her back to the ruin of black smoke billowing from the church and the gunfire in the distance behind her. She is no longer startled by the shots as when they woke her this morning, for there has been intermittent gunfire ever since. This just serves to illustrate, she thinks, listening to the latest burst of shots from somewhere behind her, how you adapt to circumstances, even when the circumstances are out of control.

The trail to the Indian camp breaks out of the poplars into a field that hints of spring in the sight ahead: George Dill and his dog, running alongside each other, a small spaniel jumping playfully at his master's leg. Dill thrusts his head back and pumps his arms wildly, running full out now, the dog bounding and snapping excitedly at his leg, the dog believing this all a game, and perhaps it is, for all around Dill lead zips and thunks softly into the spongy wet spring ground and he is almost there, almost to the cover of the bushes beyond the edge of the field when a bullet spins him around and sends him toppling backward into the poplars.

Two men run past her.

"Don't shoot!" one of them screams as his hat flies from his head and she sees by the shock of his white hair that it is

Charles Williscraft, the old carpenter, helpless and bare-headed, running for his life, "Oh, don't shoot!"

She turns in the direction of the firing to see a rider aim down on her husband.

"I am shot," he says, and staggers away from her, then turns and stumbles back, clutching his chest with both hands.

His legs crumple as she catches him under his arms, his weight pulling her down.

"I am so sorry," he says.

"Hold still," she soothes, cradling him in her arms.

Slumping forward, his chin on his chest, he watches her unbutton his blood-soaked shirt to a chest wound percolating air and blood, and it is the last thing he sees, his life slipping away, so warm, as it seeps across the back of her hand touching the wound, the small splintered fragments of bone between her fingers.

Leaning over him, she sets his head on the ground and, unable to look at his eyes, glances up for the first time since the shooting and sees no one standing in the field. No one. Just the dog at the edge of the field, tail wagging, head poked into the bushes where Dill fell. If she gets up she too will surely be shot. She is afraid to move. There is nothing she can do but lie here beside a dead man and let the cold ground seep into her.

The dog whimpers and sniffs at Dill's body and lets out a long low whine that builds to a howl, then turns and lopes across the field to discover the others. Each time it finds a body, it turns in a frenzy on its hind legs, yelping incessantly.

She flinches as a Cree wheels on his horse, takes aim, and with a single shot silences the dog. Clenched tightly against the body of her dead husband, she watches through squinted, almost-closed eyes as the riders move toward her. Criss-crossing the field they weave in and out among the corpses, so close the hooves shake the ground.

A rider reins in, his horse hovering right over her. Its nostrils nuzzle under her arm, its breath brushes down her back. She must lie perfectly still, but can't, soaked through to her skin, trembling so with fear and cold. At the first touch of hands on her back she scrambles to her feet, moving away in terror from an astonished Cree who stands and stares after her.

She trips and stumbles over Father Marchand's leg. A young Indian boy tears dead grass from the ground and, wadding it into a ball, daubs at the gash in the priest's throat. The priest struggles to get his breath, choking on his own blood.

"Tesqua! Tesqua!" At the edge of the field an old man waves his arms and shouts in Cree, "Stop! Stop!" But Big Bear has no control here. Events have taken on a volition and momentum of their own. Ignoring their chief, the men move in on her, tightening their circle till it seems she will be trampled. From the height of their horses, they loom over her, bodies painted yellow, porcupine quills jutting from black hair daubed with clay, feathers dangling from braids, faces streaked and dotted with black paint stare down at her.

Terrified, she backs away, desperately thrusting her hands in front of her as if to somehow push herself entirely from this field of slaughter, careful where she steps, looking over her shoulder to avoid tripping over another body . . .

"Theresa! Theresa!"

It is the Delaney woman, fifty feet away, kneeling between her dead husband and the black-robed body of Father Fafard. "Over here, Theresa!" she calls, standing up. They run to each other and in the comfort of their embrace shield themselves from the mounted Indians who surround them. Stopped by the women, the warriors lean out over their horses and watch them hold each other. They speak quietly in Cree while their idle horses stamp the melting snow and bend to snatch the grass uncovered by their hooves, in this the first moment of calm after the killings. Then a rider breaks from the circle, and shouting, waves his rifle across the creek to the Indian camp.

"Close your eyes and keep moving, Theresa," whispers the Delaney woman, still holding her, then breaking their embrace. "Be brave, for the water will be cold as ice."

Theresa Gowanlock holds her skirts high above water up to her knees, so cold the current cuts into her legs, numbing them until she can't move. She stands stock still in the middle of the creek, the cold current rushing against her legs. It comes to her now, as if she hears through the shock of the murders, his last words, spoken to her minutes ago, now, for the first time: he was sorry. He has left her alone in the world with his name, left her alone in this, and all he could say was he was sorry.

Someone is calling her name.

But Theresa Gowanlock cannot move out of the creek. There is nowhere to go. On one side, a field filled with corpses; on the other side, the Indian camp. No, she will simply stand here in the middle of the creek where it is safe.

A broken branch from an overhanging poplar floats by. She turns to watch it diminish downstream, a distant speck that bobs on the water, then disappears altogether. She has become that small branch, a broken twig connected to nothing, caught in the eddies of a powerful current.

Someone is calling her name.

Stunned, she stands in the frigid water, the current pulling at her legs, refusing to move, realizing in the first minutes after the killings, what has happened. The shock recedes enough for her to regain a vague awareness, someone calling her.

"Tess! Tess!" the Delaney woman calls from the far shore. "Whatever are you doing out there?"

Beyond the creek, wisps of blue smoke drift upward between the lodgepoles of the Indian camp.

Theresa Gowanlock slowly moves forward through the water toward the women she first saw on the bridge at Battleford.

A NOTE FROM CAMERON

Cold Lake, April 3, 1885

Thirty-five miles north of the Frog Lake settlement, Henry Halpin tramped the shores of Cold Lake, hoping to flush a duck. Despite the fact that Halpin returned to his cabin and Hudson's Bay store empty-handed, it remained a beautiful day. He sat outside waiting for the Chippeweyan boy he employed as a servant to cook his supper, fish again, and watched the sun drop behind the spruce, streaking the western sky orange and pink, beautiful but lonely.

For some days now Halpin had been expecting the arrival of Indians from Frog Lake to saw lumber and build flat-boats to haul freight down Beaver River. The river would soon be navigable and Halpin wondered where his men were. Spring break-up on the river was making Halpin restless, but his thoughts were interrupted suddenly by the sound of voices. Looking up Halpin saw six Indians riding toward him out of the trees.

Halpin poked his head in the doorway and said to his boy, "You'd better prepare more. Looks like we have guests for supper."

The young Indian only turned and gave Halpin an odd look that seemed unexpectedly defiant for a servant, though Halpin scarcely paid attention as he rushed outside to greet his visitors.

As the Crees rode nearer Halpin noticed something un-usual about their horses, the markings, the way they were groomed, even the way they moved. They were not Indian ponies. At least three of the Cree were riding horses he recognized as belonging to the police and the Indian Agency. Something was wrong, though Halpin had no way of knowing what, and as the riders dismounted and shook his hand they certainly seemed in good enough humour.

"I am glad to see you," Halpin said. "Have you come to build the flat-boats?"

"No," replied Lone Man, who seemed to be in charge. "We have not come to work, just to visit."

By this time Halpin's servant was outside and as the Indians laughed and joked with Halpin one of them took the boy aside and spoke quietly to him. When they came back Halpin could tell the boy had heard something to startle him, for he trembled with excitement.

"What's the matter?" Halpin asked, following the boy inside.

"You'll soon find out!"

And with an insolence Halpin no longer could ignore, the young Indian grabbed the trader's rifle off the wall, pulled on his coat, and said, "I'm going out!"

"I told you to hurry and get supper for the men," Halpin said.

But the boy only stalked out the door, rifle in hand, and without even looking back, said, "I'm going to get the horses!"

This was too much for Halpin. He stormed out of the house after the boy, his mind made up to pound some sense into him. "I told you to get supper for the men!" he shouted.

The boy ignored him and kept walking down the road.

Furious, Halpin lunged forward, seized him by the coat, and grabbing the rifle, threw it on the ground.

"Take care," the boy snarled, unintimidated by Halpin's fist raised to slam his face. "You might get into trouble."

This only infuriated Halpin more. He coiled his whole body behind his fist and at the exact moment he was set to strike, Lone Man, who had come up quietly behind them, said, "Let the boy go get the horses. There is something I want to tell you in the house."

Halpin dropped his fist. Something was wrong. He was no longer in control. He walked back to the house with Lone Man while the boy, recovering his new-found nerve, picked up the gun and went to get the horses.

When Lone Man and Halpin walked inside Halpin's small house and store, the trader found the others drinking tea fortified with his stock of Perry Davis Pain Killer.

"You have no business touching anything in the house without asking my permission," he said. "I'm in charge here."

The Crees all sat down except Lone Man. He said, "You have been a good friend of mine, and also of the others, since you came here last fall. We all like you."

This was reassuring, thought Halpin, now more confused than ever.

"We want you to tell us what you would do in case there was any trouble with the white people and the police," Lone Man said, trying to broach the subject delicately. "Which side would you take? We would like to know now before we return to Frog Lake."

Before Halpin could come up with an appropriate answer, and he couldn't, one of Lone Man's companions stood up with more questions.

"What do you think of Louis Riel? Would you help him if he were fighting the police?"

This all seemed too hypothetical for Halpin, who knew nothing of the killings and the outbreak of hostilities in the south.

"Look here," he began, but before he could say anything else, Halpin was distracted by sounds behind him and turning around saw two of the Crees changing their blanket coats for coats from the store. "Take them off!" Halpin demanded.

"No," the Indian coolly replied, refusing to take off the coat. "Everything in the country belongs to us now!" As proof of his statement, the owner of the newly acquired coat handed

Halpin a note written on a scrap of paper torn from the flyleaf of a book.

"What's this then?" demanded Halpin, holding the note in his hand.

But there was only silence in the room, as the Crees, none of whom could read what was written on the note, yet each knowing what it said, waited for Halpin to read it.

> *Dear Halpin,*
> *The Crees are going out to see you. They have killed all the white people here. Don't offer any opposition to them. They say they will not hurt you.*
> *W.B. Cameron*

The shock of Cameron's message hit Halpin with startling clarity.

The Indians consoled him with a third round of handshakes.

"You are safe with us," Lone Man reassured, "as long as you do what we tell you and promise not to try and get away. Besides," he added, "there is no place for you to go to because all the whites have been killed. If you do try to get away we will shoot you."

"Well," Halpin said, trying to recover and not doing a very good job of it. "Well, well, well..." he muttered, while the others looked at him oddly.

Just then the boy, who had returned with the horses and put them in the stable, walked back into the house.

"Well," Halpin began again. "You are my guests and you have not eaten." He turned to the boy. "Make some bread for the men. They have had nothing to eat."

"You must do the cooking now," the boy said.

THIRTY DOLLARS AND A HORSE

Big Bear's Camp, April - May, 1885

She opens her eyes, focusing from the enveloping darkness of the tipi to the small patch of sky above it. Her feet are numb and she can vaguely feel someone unlacing her shoes, pulling them off, hands peeling away her wet stockings, fingers fumbling under her soaked dress.

Someone places a fur robe over her shoulders, but she is too cold and frightened to feel its touch, soft as rabbit, on her skin. A scrap of meat speared through the sharpened point of a stick stabs at her out of the dim interior of the tipi. She opens her mouth to scream, then sees she is being offered food. She shakes her head, cringing from the dripping meat until her back touches the canvas-walled enclosure of the tipi. She is trapped, a prisoner.

A half-breed who had worked for her husband at the mill has bought her from the Crees for thirty dollars and a horse.

She doesn't understand how such a thing came about, but she knows what he wants, and is determined he shall not have it.

As soon as the Frog Lake killings started Peter Blondin set out for their house at the mill and the next day rode into camp with the Gowanlocks' wagon loaded with all of their furniture and provisions he could pile onto it. She had longed for familiar things, but now that Blondin has brought back some of their possessions she sees it is not as deep a desolation to be without them, as to watch these horrid men pull out of their dirty sacks objects and clothing she holds precious and haggle over them.

She can't stand to watch them argue and scrap over her husband's clothing. She steps outside the tent and a man standing with his back to her causes her to suffer the cruellest of illusions. A total stranger wears her husband's coat and pants, but she catches a fleeting glimpse of John in him. Peter Blondin turns and laughs in her face for he knows what she is thinking. She must get away from him quickly, now.

He has everything arranged for her to live with him – all her husband's things, all her things, and a tent. She has become one of the spoils of war, a chattel, a piece of goods sold for thirty dollars and one horse. She must escape this. Her only hope is to appeal to the mercy of John Pritchard, who has already taken in the Delaney woman.

"Yes, Mrs. Gowanlock, you can share my tent with myself and my family," he tells her. "I will protect you."

She had not seen Theresa Delaney since wading through the icy water of the creek, but now they are both together again with the Pritchards. She is safe, at least for the present, though Blondin is never far out of sight, waiting his chance. She knows there are other survivors. But where, and who? The Delaney woman tells her Cameron is alive, though she has not seen him.

Excitement spreads through the camp as six riders make their way between the tipis, horses laden with trading goods from the Hudson's Bay store at Cold Lake, the rest of the trading post piled high in a wagon driven by a young Indian. Soaked, mud-splattered and cold, Henry Halpin staggers behind the wagon, jerked along on ten feet of rope at the pace of the boy driving. The wagon stops and the Indians rush it as Halpin sinks to the ground.

A week after the murder of her husband there is to be a birth in the camp. Men have been excluded from the tipi and four women watch over the pregnant woman within. The tipi itself takes on a presence palpable to everyone in the camp and even she, watching from a distance, is touched in some way she doesn't understand.

The creased and wrinkled face of an old woman emerges, delegating errands, dispatching women to fetch things. When one of them returns with a bundle wrapped in cloth, the old woman clutches it to her withered breasts and turning, stoops to re-enter the tipi.

This is unlike anything Theresa Gowanlock has ever known. Each person in the camp, herself included, seems connected through some mystical thread with the woman about to give birth. Or perhaps it is simply that in this communal life there is no room, no physical space for privacy, and an awareness of each other's presence is heightened. Still, there is mystery in this birth and she is captivated, drawn to it in ways she herself does not understand. She watches the women prepare the moss bag, carefully cutting two holes in a piece of cotton flannel for the baby's feet; she wonders how they knew her time had come. Then, as they fold the flannel over, fine leather looped through the sides, the cloth so close she can reach out and touch it, she knows. By the faces of the moon this woman will have her baby; a period at full moon, the periods stop, and now in the tenth moon, this. As Theresa Gowanlock stands quietly outside the tipi, a part of her is inside, with the pregnant woman ... the old lady holds her around the chest from behind while another woman bears down on her, pushing; the midwife kneels between her legs, another wipes her forehead ... the startled squall of the first cry of life breaks from the tipi and then is hushed.

The women wash the baby, wrap the afterbirth, and set aside the cord to dry and hang in a beaded case round the child's neck. Finger by brown finger, two tiny fists unfold into hands small and complete. The mother pulls a print gown over the baby's head and sets it in the moss bag, the arms and legs straight and covered with heated moss, wrapped tightly in the flannels.

The brown face of a beautiful baby girl peeps out of the moss bag at Theresa Gowanlock, who is suddenly aware of her own barrenness. She is overwhelmed by a terrible loneliness she knows has come to stay. Never again will she feel the sweet nudge of her husband's knees as his body curls into hers in sleep. There is nothing now but memory.

She lifts the lid of her trunk and looks into all that remains of the short life she knew with him, all that remains of her past. Her hands rummage through the trunk, searching for something to hold on to, but all she can find is the cotton lace trimmings she so carefully crocheted through the winter, meaningless to her now. Yet she must go on. She will make a dress for the child, borrow a scrap of muslin from the Pritchard woman and sew the trimmings onto the dress.

The men have been gone from the camp for days now. What a relief to be free of their constant stares. The women govern and run the camp, gathering food, firewood, looking after children, tending animals. The old woman stoops at the side of the lake to pick up a piece of wood which she crooks in her arms. The mother bends over a brass pot and dips her spoon into a simmering gruel, the baby on her back.

She herself has been charged with making bannock. She must dig out a hole in the side of the bank and start a fire. She stirs water into the flour and kneads it hard, then flattens the dough and places it in a frying pan, ready to bake.

Later she removes the frying pan and studies the result of her first effort, bannock black as the pan itself. Odd, she thinks, cutting through the burnt crust, for even a moment to believe she could make bread like these Indian women. Yet since the day she first saw them on the bridge, she has been moving toward them in ways she could never have anticipated. She tears a piece off to taste and finds under the blackened crust the chewy texture of the bannock. Next time she will watch the fire more closely.

The chant of the camp crier rises and falls in undulating Cree: the men have returned from Fort Pitt flushed with victory. They have captured the fort, killed a policeman, taken prisoners, and allowed the police to escape downriver.

For the first time since December she sees the McLean children. They have their adventure now and revel in it. It never occurs to them that they could all be killed. But she forgets they are a family intact and unlike herself, not alone. She sees too that as Hudson's Bay factor, William McLean and his family are accorded a privileged place in the camp.

The army gains on them daily and the camp is filled with a sense of desperation, fuelled by rumours of Wandering Spirit's attempted suicide. If Big Bear's warriors say move camp immediately, then the women must tear down the tipis and move further back into the wilderness.

The men are riding horses while the women walk, their children tied to travois pulled by dogs or horses. Off she goes, walking with the Delaney woman and the Pritchard family, her thin shoes slogging through mud and water, her feet wet and sore. She has become part of a chaotic procession of howling dogs, crying babies, carts tumbling over banks, children falling, horses and oxen mired in mud, a ragged band of refugees forever moving, never arriving.

She feels numb and sick but trudges on through the bushes. Branches whip and yank her shawl. There is nothing to cover her head but a blanket and she dares not use it for fear of being mistaken for a Cree woman by one of General Strange's scouts.

They are crossing a large creek and exhausted she slumps down on a slab of rock to pull off her shoes and stockings so they will be dry when she gets to the other side. Already Kitty McLean is half-way across, water up to her waist, her three-year-old sister on her back.

She sits on an immense grey rock and takes off her shoes and stockings, not knowing what she will do next, knowing only that she can't go on. She tries to piece her thoughts together. If this is so, that Strange's scouts might mistake her for a Cree woman, who, then, would the Cree be mistaken for? The women wearing her clothes, the men, her husband's? It is all so confusing, this curious reversal of identities. She has lost everything: her pride, her identity, and now she has even lost the will and strength to go on.

She is suffering from exposure, feverish, demented. When the soldiers find her she is still sitting on this same rock, trying to tie together strands of unravelled wool that were once her shawl. Her hands tremble so badly she can't complete the knot. Her rescuers, two of General Strange's scouts, are friends of her husband from Battleford but she doesn't recognize them.

Arriving at Fort Pitt, her sense of withdrawal and isolation intensifies, for they do not stay in the fort, but board the steamer, *The North-West*. A Reverend Gordon arrives with hats and dresses. A great deal of fuss is being made over her and Theresa Delaney. On Sunday a military band sends them off to Battleford in grand style aboard *The Marquis*.

That night she stays with the Lauries with whom she had first stayed less than a year ago while waiting for her husband. He will never come now, but if he could, he would not recognize her. She has changed, utterly and completely. She wants only to withdraw, to avoid people altogether, but she and Theresa Delaney have become the focus of the entire country and everywhere their arrival is anxiously awaited.

People mean well, but she knows they cannot possibly fathom the nature of her experience. She asks herself why this happened but cannot find an answer.

No longer does she perceive them as she believed them to be, but as they are. She has lived in their lodges, eaten their food. They cared for her and kept her alive. They are a presence, a vital part of the land. Never again will she take these people for granted. When she ponders what has happened, what went wrong, a single word comes to mind: presumption.

She has lost everything, yet she cannot help wondering where the women are and whether they will ever again find a life and a home. Her experience has humbled her. Never again will she take anything for granted. Never again will she presume.

END OF THE LINE

Vancouver-New Westminster, 1948

All along the line passengers got on and off at each station and to Cameron this was quite confusing, for though it seemed he was on a train, in fact he wasn't. Yes, this outfit had a conductor with a black uniform and hat like on a train, and this rig ran on rails like a train, but instead it was one self-contained railcar that ran on electricity connected to some overhead wires. And it was all windows, huge windows, the whole upper half of the car. The modern age. He watched the furtive hurry of the passengers and thought, technology is not wisdom. Then, in the stubborn manner of an old man who shut out anything he didn't like, he pretended he was on a real train anyway. After all, he thought, settling in, opening his briefcase and pulling out a sheaf of papers and photographs as if he had all the time in the world, I am going to the end of the line.

Cameron concentrated on the photographs spread out on his lap, all men he had known in another time. They were all gone now. John Pritchard, the half-breed interpreter, passing unnoticed, except by Cameron who thought he should have been decorated a hero for protecting the two white women in Big Bear's camp. Wandering Spirit at the end of a rope in Battleford. Little Poplar in a gun fight two years later. Imasees in Montana for thirty years before getting a reservation for the people who had followed him there.

Cameron looked up from his photographs at the small boy and his young father seated across from him. To Cameron they lived in another world. Dressed in the bright stylish optimism emerging at the end of the Second World War, they would never know what he, Cameron, could never forget: that they lived and moved on this continent always at the expense of the people they had displaced. They will never see it, he thought, resting his head against the rattling window pane of the rail car, looking out at the settled countryside. Strings of new houses blurred by in the grey coastal drizzle, saddening him with the passage of time and the coming end of his own.

Of the white men at Frog Lake, Cameron alone had survived the massacre and he was eighty-three years old, a hold-over from another century, shuttling now between two cities on the Interurban somewhere between Vancouver and New Westminster. He had spent his entire life scuttling from city to city. Oh, he had tried to settle down, even to marry that girl working the dining hall of the hotel in Fort Frances. For a while she had travelled with him, once as far as Spokane, until things turned bad. She couldn't get used to his drifting from place to place, living from day to day, an itinerant hack who tried to make a living peddling his personal experiences to magazines for as little as three cents a word.

"The rate will be higher if you want the words arranged in sentences," quipped Cameron, but the editor was not amused and did not invite further submissions.

"A man proposing to make his living depending on the people who run our publications in Canada is a fit subject for a mental hospital," Cameron had once told Professor Morton.

Still, he had written the only book in existence on the Frog Lake Massacre, unless you counted those two women from Ontario who turned out that pathetic pamphlet that never would have been printed but for the fact Theresa Gowanlock's brother owned a press; that and a story someone ghosted for Eliza McLean in *The Beaver*.

It was forty-one years after the massacre when Ryerson published his manuscript in 1926. Then all he had to do was show up in any town or city with his illustrated lecture. Push the sales of the book. Give something of the events of Frog Lake and Pitt in '85. A little Indian sign language. Demonstrate a war dance. Chant some Cree. Light a fire with flint and steel. Why, it was a regular one-man Wild West show! And, of course, there were the lantern slides, the photographs . . .

Many of the photographs he was actually in himself, but then, that was what created so much interest in the book. The trick was to put in an appearance and get yourself photographed looking very much a part of things, like posing with Big Bear's twelve-year-old son, Horse Child, at Big Bear's trial. Cameron, not wearing his own clothes at all but decked out as somebody's idea of a frontiersman, complete with an absurd hat, bandana, knife in belt, hands calmly folded over the business end of a Winchester; while Big Bear's son, looking quite lost, clutched some arrows and wondered where they had taken his father. That was the best one. It proved most useful and fetched top dollar. In fact, he had forgotten how many times he had resold the same photograph and now here it was again, some sixty years later, on page five of the Saskatoon *Star-Phoenix*, a three-column feature sandwiched between an Old Virginia Pipe Tobacco ad and the movie playing at the Victory Theatre. BLEASDELL CAMERON, NOW 82, RETRACES PATH TAKEN BY BIG BEAR DURING REBELLION, and under the headline that same picture of him and Horse Child taken so long ago. At the Victory, John Garfield and Geraldine Fitzgerald were appearing with Walter Brennan and Faye Emerson in *Nobody Lives Forever*.

Well, that was certainly true, and it was good to see the movies had gotten something right for once, for as he pointed out to his friend Norman Luxton, movies were very much on his mind these days. Cameron had offered himself as a historical consultant to Cecil B. deMille for the movie *North-West Mounted Police*. ... *this is just a whisper, but I may be going down to Hollywood, not to stay, of course, but I'm in touch with the local man of one of the big producing companies. We had a long talk this afternoon and he would like me either to go down there or to have one of their men come up and get in touch with me. He says I've got more good stuff on the West than all of Hollywood put together. This just happened through a friend who was with me in the mink venture. He happened to have known or met this motion picture man and told him about me and he took the matter up with his headquarters and today he got all the dope from me and will be writing them what he thinks they should do. So if I can get a trip to Hollywood with all expenses paid, why I'm for it . . .*

Historical consultant, yes, that was the ticket. Let Luxton know he was keeping his hand in, had other things brewing, not nearly as desperate a situation as, in fact, it was. That way, when he tried to sell Luxton artifacts for the museum his friend was opening in Banff, he would get good prices. In the meantime he must start a project and extract some money from the History professor at the university, but he had to be careful for the professor had warned there were limits, once in a curious note at the bottom of a letter:

> *P.S. We do not wish to have a hundred applications for work like yours pour in upon us, so please make no mention of our arrangement.*

Still if it was done right — pique some interest, vague and general with just enough detail to get the good professor going. He would write him a letter. Now here was a photograph for the professor! Cameron looking quite natty in a white suit and cap and mounted on a penny farthing bicycle at the third annual Duck Lake Sports Day, 1891. And another taken that same Sports Day, still dressed in his white suit and smiling benevolently while eighteen Indians glared at the ground as if the very earth itself had forsaken them and they had come to this, forced to tolerate this dandified white man because he happened to work for the Duck Lake Indian Agency. But they only barely tolerated the white man's presence. That was the hard lesson Cameron learned that bitter night on the ice at Frog Lake so long ago. Five days later, when their tolerance ran out, they killed every white man in the settlement but himself.

He was only twenty-two when it happened, but that day became the focal point of his entire life. As a detective pieces together clues to reconstruct the circumstances of a crime, so Cameron had reconstructed each minute of that day a thousand times. Still, after all this time, what actually happened seemed so incredible he could only grasp and accept it by carrying wherever he went these small tangible shreds of the day's occurrences.

Cameron's thumb and finger rubbed the corner of the tattered scrap of folded paper he removed from his waist-coat pocket, unfolded, and read Quinn's handwriting:

> *Dear Cameron,*
> *Please give Miserable Man one blanket.*
> *Thomas Trueman Quinn*

It was not dated, there was no need; Cameron needed no mark to remember the date by.

He sat in the coach with the rhythm of the rails clacketing under him and as he read Quinn's note, a part of him was not in the coach at all, but reliving that Thursday, the day before Good Friday sixty-four years ago, when Wandering Spirit marked him for death and through a fluke set of circumstances he somehow escaped the fate of the others.

Three times that morning Wandering Spirit had tried to keep him with the others. "Why don't you go to church?" he asked, half-ordering Cameron to do so.

More insistent, the second time, barking the order at him: "Go to the instructor's house where the other whites are!"

Then exploding the third time: "I told you to stay with the other whites!"

Ah, but there was the small matter of a hat. Cameron was standing with an Indian named Yellow Bear on the hill a hundred yards from the Hudson's Bay store. "He's going with me to get a hat. The sun's hot and I have none," interjected Yellow Bear.

"Hurry back," ordered Wandering Spirit, and wheeling on his horse, galloped up the hill to Quinn's place.

A hat seems sane enough in all this madness, thought Cameron, walking to the Hudson's Bay store with Yellow Bear. The church was burning, the other whites were being herded into the field, and Yellow Bear, moved by some unaccountable whim, fancied a hat from the Bay store. Cameron turned the key in the door and, looking back over his shoulder, the last thing he saw before he and Yellow Bear stepped inside was Wandering Spirit and Quinn facing each other on the crest of the hill. Yellow Bear began removing hats from the shelf, studiously trying each one on as if he had all the time in the world and nothing more important to do with it.

A loud rap on the door was followed by the entrance of Miserable Man, who silently thrust a note out from his huge bulk so Cameron could read it. It was the note from Quinn authorizing Cameron to give Miserable Man one blanket.

"I have no blankets," Cameron told him.

At length Miserable Man agreed to accept a shawl, some tea, and a twist of tobacco as a substitute. He was holding a corner of the shawl in each hand so that it formed a sack-like pouch into which Cameron was dropping first the tea and now the tobacco. A brown twist the size of a carrot, the tobacco landed softly in the pocket of the shawl at the precise moment the first shot, muffled by distance and the walls of the store, reached the three men inside.

Behind the counter, Yellow Bear stared into the upturned empty crown of the hat. Miserable Man froze, his pitted face inches from Cameron's, the eyes of both men locked as they counted off each crack of the rifle. On the third shot Miserable Man sprang into action. Quickly closing the shawl and tying the tea and tobacco in a bundle, he bolted from the shop. Cameron and Yellow Bear followed to the open doorway and searched the hillside where Wandering Spirit and Quinn had been standing. Wandering Spirit was riding down the hill, yelling in Cree to his followers in the field below. Quinn lay dead on the ground. As Cameron folded the note Quinn had written him minutes ago, it was easy to imagine what had happened, Wandering Spirit ordering Quinn to join the others, just as he had ordered Cameron, Quinn refusing. The only difference between himself and Quinn was that Quinn did not have Yellow Bear to intervene. Quinn was dead and Cameron wasn't. The hat from the Bay store was just a pretext for Yellow Bear to get him away from Wandering Spirit and save him from the murders. The kindly Cree gripping Cameron by the wrist wasn't even wearing a hat now. "We must get you to the camp. Come this way," he urged.

Somewhere just outside New Westminster Cameron fell asleep.

In his dream Yellow Bear was guiding him through a field of corpses.

"End of the line, oldtimer!" The conductor tried to shake the old man awake.

Yellow Bear was taking Cameron to the safety of the neutral Woods Cree camp. When they were crossing the field after the shootings, Cameron insisted they stop to examine the corpses. He recognized George Dill's boots as they walked toward the body that lay face down in the field, the toes of his boots pointing inward and almost touching, heels angled out in the form of a V. Cameron turned him over, the face frozen in an expression of shocked surprise by the bullet that had stopped Dill in the back. Brown blades of last year's grass, twigs, and flecks of dirt were pressed into his forehead. As he looked into the lifeless face of his friend and former partner, Cameron wondered why he alone was spared.

"End of the line!" The conductor shook the old man again. Jesus — papers and photographs strewn all over the seat. The old guy must have fallen asleep. "End of the line!"

Cameron began to emerge from, while trying to recall and sustain, his dream. "Why me?" he wondered out loud.

The conductor had no idea what the old man was talking about. "You'll have to get off now," he said.

The British Columbia Electric Railway interurban trolley clanked and shunted into its New Westminster terminal.

Where was he? Banff? Yes, that was it. Going to see his friend Norman Luxton. He pressed his face against the window and looked out into the terminal. No, certainly not Banff. Cameron was too proud to ask the conductor where he was and even if he knew, he wouldn't know *why* he was here. Not that it mattered. He was an old man living from day to day, hand to mouth, on the move so many years now that everything had begun to blur into a desperate sameness. Well, thought Cameron, scooping the newspapers and photographs off the seat and stuffing them in his briefcase, it would certainly all come clear with time.

Confused, and not yet fully awake, he was just stepping down off the train with a leather bag in one hand and a briefcase stuffed with papers in the other. God, it was awkward, being a one-man travelling medicine show, packing everything with him everywhere he went. He'd actually done that in the thirties, hawked medicine, but he was on top of things again now because after all this time the book was about to be reprinted, thanks largely to Luxton.

Look at that, pure heaven: the coal black, brushed-out hair of a woman standing with her back to him in the terminal. No harm in looking, surely. That was all he'd been able to do for over fifteen years, just look. A little like getting on a train and forgetting where he was going, and why, but hoping it would come to him eventually.

Now as he stood at the top of the step-well, he realized he was not on the train, but on a trolley in New Westminster. No doubt something would soon trigger his remembering why he was here.

She turned toward him and he was looking at her as he stepped down from the trolley and felt, too late, his descending foot miss the step. He flung his hand with the briefcase out in front of him to brace the fall; his head struck the concrete.

A small crowd was gathering. He could feel people hovering over him, but he couldn't move, couldn't get up. Someone was calling an ambulance.

In the hospital again, this time the Department of Veterans Affairs in New Westminster. How embarrassing, and worse, he didn't know how he'd gotten here. He had a concussion, a sore ankle, and the doctor talked about a bruised kidney, whatever that was. Well, he felt perfectly fine, and if they insisted on keeping him here for a few weeks, he'd just catch up on his correspondence and get some work done.

First there was Luxton. He wanted to send Norman some artifacts for his Indian museum in lieu of payment on loans his friend had made to him, a delicate matter which he would approach indirectly so that it never seemed he was selling the artifacts to Luxton, even though he really was.

Dear Norman:

This will be a short letter for the light is bad. I am writing you from the hospital where I have been momentarily detained with nothing more serious than a sore ankle. I don't know how I hurt it unless it was getting on and off those crowded street cars. You come down on the hard pavement like a ton of brick, but don't worry, I'm on the mend and expect to get out of here soon.

While I think of it, I want to send you a big well-made and inlaid Sioux redstone pipe, and also, a beaded coup stick. I will be sending you the pipe and coup stick this week and I hope to square up your loan to me soon. I saw the other day that some Indian Institute or organization in New York had paid $500 for an Indian pipe.

Please excuse this terrible scrawl which I hope you can read. I've forgotten how to write with a pen and this is the worst fountain pen but the only one I could get a hold of here in the hospital.

Well Norman, old friend, all the best to you.

Heartily yours,

W.B. Cameron

Sending Norman a few things to put in his Banff Indian Trading Post would help keep the peace. Even if he couldn't pay off his debt in cash, Cameron could fill Luxton's entire museum with artifacts; he'd been trading with the Indians for years. Long before people like Luxton were opening their Indian Trading Post in Banff, Cameron had been at the vanguard of white collectors. Once the Indians had been conquered and swindled out of their land, there was nothing left to take from them but their culture. Hell, it made sense in a warped kind of way, and no sooner had the hostiles surrendered than Cameron was back in the Indian camp with a trading outfit and in one day secured most of their saleable property.

Once a trader, always a trader, and when he'd accumulated all their possessions and the Indians had nothing left to trade, why he became a journalist. For what does a journalist do but live off what happens to other people? And Cameron was right there for all of it, even the hangings. His was the only authentic eyewitness account of the massacre and its aftermath. He was there. That's what made it such a fine piece of frontier journalism.

And now, after all these years, Luxton and some people in Calgary were having the book reprinted. Why, then, was he now having second thoughts about it all? He had made the fatal mistake of writing about himself, his actual experiences, his life, and now in his final years he wondered whether in so doing, he had not somehow cheapened and diminished it.

For years the massacre had remained a mystery to him. No matter how he looked at the killings, they didn't make sense. Once while editing a newspaper in Bassano he met an old Blackfoot woman who claimed religion was at the root of the massacre: Wandering Spirit's behaviour in the church, the killing of the priests, the burning of the church. They were testing the white man's religion, testing its power. But the woman herself had been raised by nuns and later became involved in Native religion, so naturally her point of view would be religious. No, there was no rational explanation for the killings at Frog Lake.

So it had seemed. But lately his perspective was changing, his sympathies shifting. He was beginning to see things differently. A selfish and corrupt government intent on pushing the railroad through and pushing Big Bear and his people off the plains. Delaney and Quinn had cooked up a scheme that had the Indians clearing land they planned to sell for homesteads. Gowanlock would take the logs at his mill.

Then too, Delaney abused his power as Farm Instructor to take advantage of Indian women. When the husband of one of the women protested, a man named Sand Fly, John Delaney trumped up charges of assault against him, had him imprisoned, and then cohabited with his wife all winter. To add insult to injury, when he tired of the Indian woman, Delaney married a white woman, Theresa Delaney.

So the massacre. The provocation, Cameron concluded, while it did not excuse, was some mitigation of the wrongdoings.

Still, no point in brooding about it now; he had another letter to write. When Cameron stayed in a hotel he was in the habit of taking as much hotel stationery as he could lay his hands on, and then using it indiscriminately. As most of Cameron's letters were about money, the first thing he had to do was cross out the letterhead and address on the stationery. Otherwise the desired funds ended up sitting in some mail slot in a hotel lobby thousands of miles from where he actually was. Cameron reached into the bag on his table and pulled a sheet of paper from a substantial stationery collection that spanned the many years he had kicked around the country.

Rates $1.50 and $2.00   Fully Licensed
      Per Day   Free Bus
With Private Bath   HOTEL ALEXANDRA   All Modern
       $2.50   Conveniences
Telephone M 4671

FIREPROOF

F.G. Hughes and H. Corry, Lessees and Managers

Calgary, Alta.

As Cameron struck out the address on the letterhead, he realized the stationery was exactly twenty-four years older than the date he was now writing on it.

He must now include an address where he would be able to receive a reply two weeks from now. Where would he be? Still in the hospital? Or in Banff... Calgary... Regina... Saskatoon? He didn't know and the doctors would give no indication of when he would be released.

Cameron placed the pen and paper on the night table, lay back in his bed, and turned out the light. Then it came to him.

It didn't matter anymore.